"You killed men before. I read it in your eyes."

"I fought in the War," Slocum said, his mind touching on all the times he had crouched atop a hill, squinting for the glint of sunlight against Yankee braid. Kill the officers, kill the enemies' will to fight. He'd shot down more bluecoat officers than he cared to remember, but remember them he did. Each and every one. At times like this, in his darkest nightmares, he remembered.

"Somethin's botherin' you bad," said the roustabout. "And I don't think it's guilt about shootin' down Cap'n Sam. You didn't do it, did you?"

Slocum shook his head. "We all carry things in our head we'd as soon not. Sam's death isn't something I'm going to forget—and it's not going unavenged. I'll find out who's responsible and do what's necessary."

"Sure am glad I don't have nothin' to do with it, no suh . . ."

S0-BNJ-667

OTHER BOOKS BY JAKE LOGAN

JAKE LOGAN

SLOCUM'S PRIDE

BERKLEY BOOKS, NEW YORK

SLOCUM'S PRIDE

A Berkley Book/published by arrangement with
the author

PRINTING HISTORY
Berkley edition/December 1984

ISBN: 0-425-07567-2

A BERKLEY BOOK ® TM 757,375
Berkley Books are published by Berkley Publishing Group,
200 Madison Avenue, New York, NY 10016.
The name "BERKLEY" and the stylized "B" with design
are trademarks belonging to Berkley Publishing Corporation.

PRINTED IN THE UNITED STATES OF AMERICA

1

Captain John Slocum, late of the C.S.A., lost the two poorly dressed men who were following him in the bustling crowd near the New Orleans docks by cutting unexpectedly from Canal Street to Julia Street. He had no idea who they were, but he knew he didn't want to find out. Anything out of the ordinary meant only potential trouble for him. The War had been over a scant three years, and he still hadn't adjusted properly to life in the Reconstructed South. The damn carpetbaggers meddled and stole indiscriminately, and the Northern politicians kept sending more and more of them down every month. Slocum didn't rightly know where they'd all end up if something wasn't done to stem the flow—and soon.

He ducked into a small cafe a few blocks away from the Girod Street landing and settled into a hard, straight-backed chair from which he could see anyone entering in the grimy mirror hanging along one wall.

"What'll it be?" the waitress drawled, turning single syllables into what she thought was a sexy, intimate tone. She eyed him impudently, even wantonly. At another time Slocum might have been tempted, but now all he felt was hollowness inside.

He had done his part for the Confederacy, and all it had got him was shot up and hunted like a wild animal. Riding with Quantrill had been nothing less than a continual commitment to viciousness and cold-blooded killing that had worn on him until Slocum knew he couldn't take it any longer. Getting gutshot—and by men who were supposed to be on his side—had been lucky, though Slocum had hardly seen it that way at the time, being at death's door for months and requiring even longer months to recuperate. He hadn't been able to stomach what Quantrill and Bloody Bill Anderson had done at Lawrence, Kansas.

War was war, and Slocum hated it, but what they did was cruelty for the sick thrill of being cruel. They'd taken care of him in their own way, and Slocum had spent the rest of the War trying to keep from dying in a lonely shack.

"Steak and eggs," he ordered. "Coffee."

"Got chickory," the waitress said, putting one hand on her hip and cocking it outward toward Slocum. "That good enough for the likes of you?" Her face went hard when Slocum paid her no heed. He was too busy looking in the mirror to see if the men on his trail had sniffed out his scent again. They had the look of federal marshals about them; he had seen that look often enough in the past few years.

Getting home to Calhoun County after healing up some had been his only goal. His brother Robert had died in the War and his parents had also passed on. Slocum wanted nothing more than to settle down, farm, and try to forget.

"Damn judge," he mumbled.

"What's that, honey?"

"Nothing. Don't burn the steak. I want it so rare it lows when I stick a fork into it."

She sniffed and left. Slocum's hand went to the ebony

grip of his Colt Navy when two men entered the cafe. They had the look of the law about them. Slocum tried to keep still when he saw a battered tin badge on the tall, skinny one's vest. They sat down across the room and began joking with the waitress, their eyes only on her. Slocum relaxed a mite.

Not everyone recognized him as the man who had gunned down a carpetbagger judge and the judge's hired gun. The judge had taken a fancy to Slocum's farm and had told him no taxes had been paid on the land during the War. Pay up or get out, the judge had ordered.

Even if Slocum had had the money, he wouldn't have paid the extortion. That kind of kowtowing didn't set well with him, then or now. The judge and the gunhand had come to throw Slocum off the farm.

Two fresh graves stood on the ridge overlooking a pleasant meadow by the time Slocum rode out. He had burned the house, the two barns he had worked so hard to restore, and the springhouse. Along with them went any chance he had for a normal life. Judges hate judge killers, even when the dead are crooked sons of bitches. Slocum had ridden hard, getting back to the West and the frontier where people kept their own counsel and didn't ask damn fool questions about matters that didn't concern them.

"Here's your food, mister," the waitress said. "Hope you don't choke on it."

Slocum smiled at that and got an almost shy smile in return. The waitress turned and went off, flouncing and giving him the eye again. Slocum ate in silence, barely tasting the food. He hadn't been long enough in New Orleans to see much of the city, but there'd be other times, times without marshals breathing down his neck. He finished and dropped four bits on the table. Slocum tipped his hat to the waitress as he left. The two men at the other table never even glanced in his direction.

Feeling better for having eaten, he walked quickly to the docks to seek out a way north, maybe as far north as St.

Louis. Wanted posters got around faster than a man could run, but nobody'd expect him upriver. Not if reports had been sent placing him in New Orleans.

Along the wharves, Slocum stopped and stared, open-mouthed. A sternwheeler had docked at the Girod Street landing while he ate. The paddle box on the side had been painted garishly with an armored English knight swinging a gleaming sword. Bannered behind the knight with the sword in bright red lettering was the name *Excalibur*.

"If'n you keep your mouth open like that, John, you'll be catching enough flies to go fishin' again," said a voice.

"Samuel Jackson! You old—" Slocum began.

"Watch your language, you young whippersnapper. It's *Captain* Jackson now."

"So I see." Slocum looked at his old friend. Samuel Jackson and he went back a long way, back to their childhood days in Georgia. Sam had been ten or twelve years older and had left to make his mark in the world. Slocum had seen him twice during the War, both times running arms and supplies to starving, chronically ill-supplied Southern troops in Kansas and Arkansas. But Sam had been only a deckhand then, straining to move the bales and barrels before the Union cavalry had a chance to ride up and put a few extra holes in both ship and crew.

"Time's treating you with a kind hand, John. You're fit as a fiddle." Jackson glanced over his shoulder and said in a lower voice, "And as high strung."

"Some things don't change." Slocum didn't have to explain to the riverboat captain. Jackson nodded and motioned for Slocum to join him aboard the *Excalibur*. Slocum noticed that Jackson wasn't exactly the calm sort, either. He made many nervous gestures with his eyes, looking this way and that, as if expecting to find someone eavesdropping on him.

"A fine ship, my *Excalibur*," the man said proudly. "But living on it gets to me now and then. Didn't used to be like that, not in the old days. Didn't use to be a river man, either."

"You fixing to push on soon?" Slocum asked. He had some thought of being aboard the *Excalibur* when the ship sailed. He needed to get out of New Orleans, and what better way of going than this floating pleasure palace?

Jackson sat behind a huge mahogany desk in his office just off the boat's long ballroom and poured himself a shot. He knocked it back, poured another, and then offered Slocum one.

"You're quick with the compliments," said Slocum, wondering at the man's case of nerves. "I look like I been dragged through the knothole backwards. Been riding harder than hell for over two weeks and—"

"Who's after you?" Jackson asked quickly. Even more quickly, he held up his hand and went on, "Don't make no never mind to me. Don't especially want to know. If you need a ride, you got it. I'll have a cabin fixed up special for you. The *Excalibur* always has room for one more."

Slocum looked around the cabin and took a deep breath. Compared to the nickel-a-night hotel he was holed up in, this was heaven. The rich walnut paneling had been polished to within an inch of its life, the furnishings were more likely to be found in some rich man's parlor than on board a riverboat pulled up to a New Orleans dock, and the forest-green rugs on the floor felt sinfully soft beneath Slocum's boots. It wouldn't be hard for him to get to like living in such surroundings.

"I never asked for charity before, and I'm not now. I'll work my way to wherever you're going."

Sam Jackson's expression defied words. Slocum had expected one of two responses. Either Jackson would tell him to go stake out a bunk below deck with the crew or he would say that, for old times' sake, Slocum would be riding in first class. Slocum would have been satisfied with sleeping on deck with the stowage passengers if it meant getting away from the men so aggressively following him.

But Jackson just sat and stared out the beveled glass window looking onto the river. Slocum would have bet his last greenback that the captain of the *Excalibur* never even saw the fancy mermaids etched into the glass or the muddy riverbank and the traffic on the Mississippi outside. Whatever was eating away at the man, it was powerful.

Slocum rocked back in the chair and finished off the remaining finger of whiskey. It burned his throat and went on down to form a warm puddle in his belly. Slocum had tasted better, but that was so long ago the memory faded.

"What do you say to a bit of duck huntin'?" Jackson asked unexpectedly. "Got a pair of fine gooseguns. Full chokes. We can blow these canvasbacks right out of the sky at a hundred yards."

"Where? In downtown New Orleans?" asked Slocum, half joking.

"Out on Lake Pontchartrain. Know the best damn spot in all of Louisiana for hunting. I go out there all the time when we're docked in New Orleans. Just the two of us, John. Like old times."

"Can't say I remember going hunting with you, Sam."

The man's expression clouded, then outright fear seized him. "Please, Slocum. I just want to get off the *Excalibur* for a while. Been cooped up on the old girl till I'm damn near ready to scream."

"Whatever you say, Sam." Slocum wasn't keen on the idea of leaving what he now thought of as the sanctuary of the riverboat, but his curiosity bump began to itch something fierce. Those federal marshals nosing around out in the city weren't likely to come upon him out duck hunting in a swamp any more than they were to find him aboard the riverboat. Maybe less likely. Slocum couldn't say.

The captain shot out of his chair and took three quick strides to a cabinet set in the wall. He fumbled for a moment with a large brass key and finally unlocked the door to reveal a brace of pistols, four Spencer carbines, and the two shotguns. Slocum took one of the shotguns and examined it.

"Nice," he said, meaning it. "Good balance. Must knock

the ducks out of the sky with every shot." The Damascus barrel had been engraved with patterns of other hunters bagging their game. Just the feel of the gun made Slocum want to go out and try it. He told Jackson.

"Let's do it, then, John,"

Slocum trailed a little behind as his friend went about the *Excalibur* performing one last check and turning over supervising the crew to his chief clerk, a surly individual with a badly scarred face from a bout of smallpox. Slocum felt the animosity between the men but said nothing about it. Everything about this sudden hunting trip struck Slocum as odd. He didn't remember Samuel Jackson as having that big a taste for fowl.

"Come along, John. Time's a-wastin'."

They went down the gangplank and soon lost themselves in the thick crowds milling around the New Orleans dock area. Slocum kept one eye open for trouble, but they arrived at the L&N Railroad station without incident.

Jackson bought tickets, saying, "We'll get off just the other side of Lake Pontchartrain. This spot I know is within a mile of the tracks. This is going to be great, John. I feel it. I been needin' something to take my mind off . . . business matters."

Slocum decided it had been too long since he'd really known Sam. As a youth, Jackson had been anything but serious-minded. It had been a local joke how the youth squandered his money in every possible way. He'd been a spendthrift, but Slocum allowed as to how a man could change. They'd all done a heap of growing up during the War.

Only when the train pulled out, heavy, oily black smoke rising from the battered smokestack, did Sam Jackson relax. He closed his eyes and tipped his head back to the top of the seat, his fingers lightly closed around his shotgun.

"You're looking better just being away from the *Excalibur*," said Slocum. "Maybe you're not the kind for being a captain. Nothing personal," he added hastily. "It just seems to me that you were as nervous as a long-tailed cat in a rocking-chair factory."

"No," said the man. "Nothing of the kind."

"You lit out like someone set fire to your coattails. You didn't even bother to change out of your uniform." Several of the other passengers had stared for a while, then turned back to their own thoughts as the train rolled along noisily. Jackson grabbed for the front of his coat and touched a packet of papers inside. Even above the clank of steel wheels on rails, Slocum heard the familiar rustling.

"Had to get away from the boat for a while," said Jackson. "You gave me a good reason. Old friend and all that."

"You're the captain. Why do you need a reason to leave your own ship? Or is the owner likely to come by and toss you off if he finds you gone?"

Jackson laughed harshly. "I'm the owner. I'm not at all sure I could fire myself, even if I wanted to. Fact is, John, I *like* being a riverboat captain. There's excitement to it. You've never lived until you get into a race with another boat. The *Excalibur* is the fastest on the river, bar none. Why, we raced the *Natchez* from St. Louis up the river to Louisville and beat her by more than ten minutes."

"Heard good things about the *Natchez*," Slocum said.

"Her captain's none other than A. L. Shotwell. He set the record from New Orleans to Louisville before the War. Fifty-three or thereabouts. Made the trip upriver in four days, nine hours. And I beat that son of a bitch.

"Yep, John, the *Excalibur*'s a sweet boat. None better. I'm damn happy to own her."

"You must have come into a powerful lot of money," said Slocum. "I remember you always having trouble hanging onto more'n two bits at a time."

"Got lucky," Jackson said, but Slocum noted the curtain had drawn back. The riverboat captain was silent about how he'd come by the money to buy such a fine vessel, and Slocum didn't press. It wasn't any of his business.

"Here. We get off here." Jackson pulled the emergency cord and the train screeched to a halt. The conductor eyed them disapprovingly as they climbed down.

"You don' go thinkin' we's stoppin' for y'all on the way back, now you heah?"

Jackson only laughed. "Don't go bad-mouthin' a pair of fine hunters like us," he said. The conductor frowned and shook his head when Jackson slipped him a folded ten-dollar bill. "Treat us right and we'll bring you a couple of those canvasbacks for your supper." The conductor snorted, indicating that he didn't think they'd be that lucky, then motioned to the engineer to get rolling again.

"They'll stop. They always do," said Jackson. He sucked in a chestful of air and exhaled. "Great spot."

Slocum looked around and wondered what Jackson saw in this particular patch of land. The swamp scum floated green and ugly on stagnant ponds. Occasional gators surfaced, one slitted, yellow reptilian eye giving them the once-over before vanishing without so much as a ripple in the water. Fragrant cypress tried vainly to overcome the stench of decaying vegetation, banyans reached out their impossibly long arms, and then let roots dip into the soft ground. Spanish moss hung like green wedding veils from the trees, slowly choking them to death with its lacy fingers. Slocum had seen worse. He'd also seen places he'd prefer to be.

They trooped along, Jackson unerringly finding the high, dry ground. Weaving through the swamp, they soon found ponds alive with ducks.

"A bit late in the morning to expect much, isn't it?" asked Slocum.

"Don't care," admitted Jackson. "There's a few things I want to tell you, John."

Slocum tensed. He didn't like anyone sharing secrets. The burden that placed on him was unwanted. He had troubles enough of his own without taking on another man's.

"The *Excalibur*. You were right in wonderin' how a man like me got enough together to buy it outright. The trade's prosperous up and down the river," Jackson said. "The *Excalibur* can haul five hundred tons of cargo at good rates. Fifty passengers at half the price of a stagecoach. Damn fine engines. Hippel & Evans made 'em up in Albany, Indiana. Couldn't be prouder of that boat. No, sir."

"You're dancing all around saying what you mean, Sam."

Darkness settled over Jackson's face. "You always were a sharp one, John. Saw into people's hearts."

They sloughed through ankle-deep water and came to a duck blind constructed out of white pine. As Jackson climbed into it, Slocum heard a distant splashing. He turned and squinted into the sun. A clump of cattails moved about, but it might have been nothing more than a stray breeze, though Slocum felt nothing of it. He frowned as the clump swayed again. Slocum's finger tightened on the shotgun's double trigger.

"What's wrong, John? Get in or you'll end up getting soaked to the bone. We should have dressed for this instead of just coming on out."

"Nothing," said Slocum. The cattails waved about again. He still didn't feel any wind. Slocum settled down into the blind beside his friend. "What are we going to do if we happen to hit something? We really need a couple of good bird dogs to make this worthwhile."

Sam Jackson chewed on his lower lip and looked even more worried than before. Slocum said nothing. He figured he'd let the man get to speaking his piece in his own time. Some men didn't cotton to being pushed, but unless Sam spoke soon, Slocum knew he'd explode.

Finally, Jackson said, "I gotta tell someone this, John." Even though the day was still moderate, a thin sheen of sweat beaded on the riverboat captain's upper lip.

"If it's anything illegal, you'd better reconsider, Sam."

"I know you got problems in that line, John. I hear a lot around the docks. Sailors got little else to do than gossip like old women."

"What did you hear?"

"The judge and his deputy, rumors of a few banks missing funds after a gunman made a quick withdrawal and even quicker getaway. But my problems are *big*, John."

Slocum knew Jackson had a habit of exaggerating. He told the biggest fish stories in all of Calhoun County, but the intensity of the man's words convinced Slocum this wasn't the case now. Whatever ate at his guts was important.

"Can I help?" Slocum frankly hoped the answer would be "no." He had a world of trouble all on his own without finding somebody else's.

"I'm hoping you can, John. See, I got myself ass deep in something that's no good for me."

Slocum's attention drifted from what Jackson was saying to a slow, deliberate sloshing sound. He half stood in the duck blind and peered out. The cattails in the distance no longer moved. He decided he was just jumpy.

"John," Jackson went on, not even noticing his momentary inattention, "I been married for seven years now. I don't see Marie—she's in St. Louis—all that much. Just a day or two while we get the *Excalibur* reloaded for the trip back downriver. But I love that woman, and she's been nagging me to give up the boat."

"You want to do that?"

"Not really. I asked Marie to come along. You seen the captain's cabin. We could live right fine aboard ship, but she won't do that. Says the smell of the waterfront makes her sick. Fact is, she just doesn't like the low-lifes who ship aboard any riverboat."

Slocum guessed Marie Jackson came from a rich family, maybe from a Northern manufacturing fortune. He also wondered how Mrs. Jackson filled her long, lonely hours when her husband was travelling on the Mississippi.

"What do you intend to do?" Slocum asked.

"That's what's got me so twisted up inside. I got involved in a deal that's gonna make me rich. I figure on retiring then, letting someone else captain the *Excalibur* while I sit back and spend my money."

A loud splash pulled Slocum back up.

"What's wrong, John? I brought you out here so I could talk to you without a lot of interruption. Hell and damnation, I didn't even expect to *see* a duck. There's them amongst my crew I don't trust."

"Get rid of them. You're the captain."

Jackson smiled ruefully. "It ain't that easy. You don't understand about the river. Some folks on a riverboat are damn near impossible to replace and if I did, it'd raise too many questions. This deal's a sweet one, John, but risky."

"You mean illegal."

"Of course it is. Nothing that'll bring me fifty thousand dollars is legal. I could run the *Excalibur* for ten years and still not make that much profit, free and clear."

"A powerful lot of money," Slocum allowed.

"John, I want you to—"

Hot lead grazed Slocum's head. He fell forward, stunned but still conscious. He toppled onto Jackson, who had taken the full load of buckshot in the chest. Slocum straddled over the riverboat captain for a few seconds, then forced himself to a sitting position. Sluggish blood trickled down the side of his head. No serious damage done, but the impact had shaken him up. Slocum swung up to his knees, the blind and the pond around whirling in crazy circles. He shoved the shotgun in front of him and saw the two men in the rowboat. One reloaded his shotgun while the other worked at the oars.

Slocum's vision was blurry, and his head hurt like a son of a bitch, but he wasn't going to let these bushwhackers get away scot free. He aimed in their general direction and pulled the first trigger. The recoil knocked him back. He got back up and gave the second barrel a better aim.

The men in the boat screeched, the one dropping his shotgun into the water. Both started rowing. By the time Slocum had reloaded and fired both barrels, the rowboat was out of sight, darting behind a clump of greenish-yellow marsh grass taller than Slocum's head.

"John," Sam Jackson called out. "Th-they got me good. I feel all tore up inside."

"You'll be all right, Sam. I'll get you to a doctor, and he can fix you up."

"No!" Sam Jackson spit up frothy pink blood. Slocum had seen enough chest wounds during the War to know this one was bad. Real bad.

"Just lie easy." Slocum tried to make his friend more comfortable, but there wasn't much he could do.

"The papers. In my pocket. They get shot up, too?"

"No," said Slocum, pulling them out. Some blood had soaked onto the envelope, but the thick sheaf of documents inside remained unscathed.

"Deed to the *Excalibur*. I want you to have 'er, John. Lemme sign 'er over now. Before I die."

"The boat rightly belongs to your . . . wife." Slocum had started to say "widow."

"Do whatever is right, John." Jackson spat blood again and fumbled out a stubby lead pencil. He carefully traced out his name on the bottom line.

"They're going to think I killed you for the boat, Sam," said Slocum.

"No, no," he said, his voice weakening. "I done wrote up what happened on the back of the deed. And they won't want no lawmen snoopin' around. Get the *Excalibur* to St. Louis. Then you— God, it's all liquid in my guts. I feel so weak."

Sam Jackson slid to the bottom of the duck blind, dead.

Slocum stared at the deed to the *Excalibur* and the explanation on the back. Any half-baked shyster lawyer could tear this to ribbons. Slocum rocked back and said, "I don't want your damned riverboat, Sam, but I will deliver it to your widow."

Slocum closed his eyes for a moment and awoke a little past noon, his head ready to explode. He forced himself to his feet, got Sam up onto his shoulders, and began trudging to the L&N Railroad line for the trip back to New Orleans.

He didn't look forward to what he had to do, either in explaining how Sam had come to be killed or in taking the *Excalibur* north to St. Louis.

But he'd do it. He had promised.

2

Slocum flagged down the train and, after five minutes of argument with the conductor, put Sam Jackson's body into the mail car. Slocum was more than content to ride there, and all the way into New Orleans his mind seethed with the problems he now faced. It wasn't enough that he had the law after him for what he'd done in Georgia. Now they'd be snooping about asking all manner of questions—and Slocum didn't know the answers.

It had to look as if he was the one responsible for murdering Jackson. Slocum knew he'd spend a long, long time in jail if he tried to get anyone to believe the alibi that was the God's truth. No marshal worth his salt would believe two men had rowed up on the pond and killed Sam, just like that. What was their motive? Who the hell were they? Slocum couldn't give those answers, because he didn't have the foggiest idea what Sam had been involved in, other than that it wasn't legal.

Slocum spat out the open door and watched the wind catch the gobbet and pull it from sight. Staying with Sam's body meant nothing but a world of trouble. He ought to jump the train right now, catch the next one going in the other direction, and keep on going.

"Can't," he said, pulling the packet of papers from his pocket and staring at them. "He deeded the *Excalibur* over to me, but the boat belongs to his widow."

Slocum knew the law was on Marie Jackson's side as far as upholding a claim on the riverboat. He also knew the *Excalibur* would never reach St. Louis unless someone was along to bird-dog it. Some sharp dealer would change the name and registration and a newly painted sternwheeler would steam into port as proud as you please, all trace of the *Excalibur* gone. Marie Jackson would be out not only a husband but all that her husband had worked for along the river.

Slocum slammed one fist into the palm of his other hand and swore long and bitter. When things turned to shit, they did it with a vengeance. Honor dictated that he see this through to the end.

Slocum quieted down and heaved a sigh. That end might be one with him looking through a federal prison's bars. He wondered what the weather was like in Detroit this time of year, then decided it would be at least another month before the fine-turning grinder of justice sent him in that direction.

Slocum looked up when the conductor came back and peered down at him, a curious expression on his wrinkled black face.

"Why fo' you still heah?" the man asked.

Slocum jerked his head in Jackson's direction. "He had a wife. Up in St. Louis. Got to see he gets a proper burial, and that she gets these." He tapped the packet of papers containing the title to the *Excalibur*.

"Boy, you're plumb crazy. They gonna flay that white skin of yours right off your bones and hang you out to dry."

"Probably."

The conductor frowned even harder and made new wrinkles furrow across his brow. "That don' bother you?"

"Bothers me a lot," Slocum said. "But I know where my duty lies. He was my friend. A long time ago."

"Befoah the War?"

Slocum nodded.

"Cap'n Jackson, he was a good man. Better'n most what rides on this heah train," the conductor said. "He been followin' around some bad men, goin' back and forth from New Orleans to heaven knows wheah." The man's eyes widened a little and the whites showed all around. "You fight in the War?"

"Under another Jackson," Slocum admitted. "Maybe that's why I feel I owe Sam something." He shook his head. "No, that's not right. He was my friend. I owe him for that."

"You with Jackson's Brigade?"

"I was. At Bull Run." Slocum spat again. He remembered the taste of the Monopole champagne they'd captured and drunk beside the stream. All of Washington society had come to see the South get its comeuppance. It hadn't worked that way, and they'd fled back to the sanctity of their city, leaving picnic lunches and cases of the sparkling wine. Slocum and his comrades in arms had drunk it that day, amid the dead covered with crawling flies and caked blood.

The conductor cleared his throat and leaned out to peer forward. "Now I don't want to be givin' out unwanted advice to a Reb veteran, but if'n you and him just happened to slip off the train when she slows down for this heah curve, you'd be less than a mile from the Girod Street landing and that fancy boat of his'n."

Slocum took a couple of seconds to understand what the conductor was saying. Then he smiled. "Thanks."

"Don't thank me, boy. Jist git your white ass off my train. I don't want to answer no questions about how no dead man came to be in my mail car."

Slocum slid to the open door and looked out. The train

slowed for the curve. He grabbed a handful of uniform and tugged Sam Jackson's body along with him. He let the motion of the train heave him outward. He jerked, and the corpse landed heavily beside him. The last Slocum saw, the conductor touched the shiny black brim of his hat, and vanished back into the mail car, ready to continue his duties.

Slocum struggled along with Jackson's body, now growing ripe in the afternoon sun. Never had he been happier than he was to see the *Excalibur*'s chimneys with their fancy wrought-iron tops or the scene of the knight wielding the magical sword for which the riverboat was named. He staggered up the gangplank and dropped Jackson's body behind a bale of cotton. Slocum turned and ran smack dab into the tall, skinny man Jackson had said was his chief clerk.

Watery blue eyes darted from Slocum to the dead captain and back. "You kill him?"

"No," said Slocum. "Be damn stupid of me to kill him and then bring him back like this, wouldn't it?"

"What happened?" The pockmarked face betrayed no hint of remorse or any other emotion. The chief clerk might as well have been checking cargo.

"Bushwhacked. We were out in a duck blind beyond Lake Pontchartrain. Two men in a boat came alongside us and opened fire. Sam got hit square. They only grazed me." Slocum's hand reached up to touch the spot where one of the lead pellets had scored his head.

The clerk dropped to one knee and began searching through Jackson's pockets.

"These what you're looking for?" asked Slocum, holding out the title to the *Excalibur*.

"Gimme those."

Slocum jerked back. The look of his cold green eyes stopped the clerk dead in his tracks.

"They don't belong to you," said the clerk. "Those are important for the running of the *Excalibur*."

"Right important, I'd say," said Slocum. "Especially

considering that they're the papers signing over the riverboat to me. Sam did it just before he died."

"Ain't legal," snapped the clerk.

"Sam wrote it out on the back of one of the pages. I think his explanation will stand up in court." Slocum saw the trapped look come into the man's pale blue eyes and decided to see how far he could push him before he balked like an old mule. "Go on and call the law. There's no reason we can't have all this straightened out before—"

"No!"

"How's that?"

"We don't need no half-assed marshals nosing about on the *Excalibur*."

"You saying that you consider this a legal document entitling me to ownership of the *Excalibur?*"

"Reckon so."

Slocum's eyes narrowed. The man was spooked now. He hadn't been at all moved by the sight of the riverboat's captain—owner dead, but the merest suggestion of getting the law involved got his back up.

"My name's Slocum."

"I'm the *Excalibur*'s chief clerk. Leander Martin."

"Maybe we ought to get the federal marshal over and let everyone know what's happened."

"No! I mean," Martin went on hurriedly, "Captain Jackson wouldn't have wanted it that way. He . . . he always wanted a burial on the river. It was his home. Ain't no business of anyone else what we do."

"Well, Mr. Martin, that sounds like the proper course." Slocum had no desire to see Jackson's body decaying further. Best to deliver the lifeless remains into the swirling yellow murk of the Mississippi once the riverboat started north toward St. Louis.

"As the new owner, I'd like to talk to the rest of the crew."

Martin glared at him and started to say something, then

bit it off. What he finally said was much milder than Slocum expected. "You're gonna need a captain, unless you can handle those chores."

Slocum laughed. "I'd just as soon go along for the ride to St. Louis," he said. "Enjoying being owner of such a fine sternwheeler is all I really want to do."

"I'll find us a captain," said Martin.

"Except," cut in Slocum, "for a few minor tasks like choosing who's to be captain. I want to protect my investment."

Martin's watery eyes coldly studied Slocum. "Of course, Slocum."

"Mr. Slocum. I am the owner of the boat now."

"Yes, sir, *Mr*. Slocum." The sarcasm cut like a knife.

Slocum ignored it. The man's behavior wasn't at all what Slocum had expected, and he didn't pretend to understand what was going on. Slocum made a guess that it had something to do with the illegal activities Jackson had mentioned out in the duck blind. Slocum didn't know much about riverboats, but he figured that the chief clerk would know what illicit cargo was being shipped. There wasn't much way he couldn't know, if he did his job.

For all the animosity Slocum felt for Leander Martin, he had to give the man his due for seeming to run a taut cargo manifest. The bales of cotton on the deck had been neatly stowed, the sugar cane forward had been lashed securely, and the decks were damn near clean enough to eat off. Nothing could be sneaked aboard without Martin knowing of it, and Martin's panic at the idea of the law investigating Jackson's murder told Slocum that whatever was being smuggled was already aboard.

"When was Captain Jackson intending to sail?" Slocum asked.

"Dawn tomorrow. We got one more load of cane coming in to give us a full cargo."

"How much is that?"

Martin sneered at the new owner's ignorance. "Pert-near

five hundred tons, all told. We're looking to make a thousand dollars' clear profit on this haul upriver."

This was a far cry from the fifty thousand Jackson had mentioned.

"How would you suggest I go about getting a new captain?"

"Since you don't want me meddlin' in *owner's* business, ain't for me to say, now is it?" The tone Martin used made Slocum fight to keep his temper. Slocum's hand twitched slightly just over the butt of his pistol.

"Show me to the captain's cabin. I need to clean up, if I'm going to be interviewing for such an important position." Slocum could barely stand himself. The stench from walking through swampy lands was bad, but the smell of death clung with even greater tenacity.

"I got work to do. Get one of the stewards," Martin said.

"No," said Slocum, his voice turning in. "You. You're going to show me around the *Excalibur* and introduce me to the crew, and you're going to tell them I am the new owner. Then you will get on with whatever it is you have to do."

"I got to check out the holds. The cargo," Martin protested.

"It's not going anywhere. Looks as if you did a good job getting it loaded so far. A few more minutes won't matter. If it does, you can try your luck on another riverboat. There's not much difference to me in finding a captain *and* and chief clerk and in just looking for a captain."

"You can't fire me! I been with Captain Jackson for over two years."

Slocum outstared Martin. The man's watery blue eyes averted, and he began shuffling his feet. Slocum decided he was off to a good start with Leander Martin. The chief clerk had learned who was in charge.

But Slocum wasn't going to turn his back on the man. Not if the way Martin glared at him meant anything.

* * *

Slocum rocked back in the captain's desk chair and lit one of the fancy havanas he found in Jackson's humidor on the desk. He let a blue cloud of smoke out of his lungs and relaxed. It had been a hell of a day, and he was glad things had worked themselves out as well as they did. He still had problems figuring out Leander Martin's reaction to seeing Sam Jackson dead, and it was downright strange the way the chief clerk accepted Slocum as the new owner with hardly a fuss.

He was hiding something, Slocum decided. There was no escaping the conclusion that it was tied into the illicit activity Jackson had mentioned just before he'd been bush-whacked. Smuggling was the obvious answer to Slocum, but his quick look at the *Excalibur* didn't turn up anything other than the cotton bales, sugar cane, and some tobacco that Martin's manifest so neatly itemized.

Slocum puffed hard until he reduced the fine smoke to ashes. Stubbing it out, he looked over the piles of paperwork on the desk. It was all his now and, as much as he'd have liked to ignore it, Slocum knew it had to be tended to. The thought of some dockmaster preventing the *Excalibur* from leaving just because the proper forms hadn't been filled in didn't set well with Slocum, but he had been in the army. He knew how petty men enjoyed showing their power over others, no matter how trivial the claim.

The door to the captain's office flew open and crashed against the wall. Slocum's reaction was instinctive. He had the Colt Navy out, cocked, and pointed at the man in the door before the last of the echo died.

"Damn it!" the dandy in the doorway cried. "What the hell kind of boat is this?"

Slocum frowned. The man wore a flashy June-bug green velvet coat with gold trim and pearl buttons, tight brown silk breeches that looked to be shrunk down to a second skin, meticulously polished black leather high-heeled boots with gold tassels, and an expression of pure disgust.

"Why are you pointing that ridiculous gun at me?" the man demanded.

"Can't say whether I ought to shoot you or stuff you into a bottle so's some professor type can tell me what you are," said Slocum.

"I'm the *Excalibur*'s pilot," the man said, pulling himself up to his full height of five foot seven. Even with the high-heeled boots, he didn't top out anywhere near as bold as he acted.

"We got two of them," said Slocum. "You must be Hank Sanders."

The pilot made a dramatic gesture, pushed a hand back through his thinning red hair, and struck a pose like a Shakespearean actor ready to deliver a speech. "*Henry* Sanders, please. And to you, it is Mr. Sanders."

"I'm the new owner," said Slocum. "You probably heard Sam Jackson met with a load of buckshot."

"Unfortunate."

Slocum snorted in disgust, lowered the hammer on his Colt, and put it back into his cross-draw holster. "Next time you want to talk with me, Hank, you can knock first and wait to be told to come in. And if I know it's you, it'll be a cold day in the swamps before I even notice you."

"I'll quit," the man threatened. "I will not be bullied or mistreated."

"Don't let the door whap you in the ass as you're leaving."

Sanders's eyes widened in disbelief. "But I'm the god-damn *pilot*. You can't talk to me like that!"

"Just did. Don't want a pilot on the *Excalibur* who's hard of hearing." Slocum watched the man's face redden with uncontrolled anger.

"You, sir, have no respect for your betters!"

"For my betters, I do," said Slocum, tiring of the dude. "For the likes of you, no. If you do your job well and don't give me any back talk, I'll consider calling you Henry. Till then, Hank, I am busy." Cold green eyes bored into the pilot, making him flush an even darker red.

"No one's ever talked to me like that," the pilot said in disbelief.

"Shouldn't you be getting ready to leave? Tomorrow at dawn the *Excalibur* is heading upriver, with or without you."

Henry Sanders turned and left without another word. Slocum frowned and muttered, "Now what was that all about?"

Replacing the dandy in the doorway was the man's exact opposite. Hair in wild disarray, cloth coat ripped in places and sorely in need of cleaning, boots exposing dirty toes, the man stroked over a three-day stubble on his chin.

"Never seen that in well nigh thirty years on the river," the man said. "I had some misgivings about coming to the *Excalibur* when I heard old Sam had been shot up, but I wouldn't mind shipping for an owner what handles those damn fool jackass pilots like you did that peacock."

"You knew Sam?"

"Not all that good. We met up a time or two in a tavern and swapped lies. Good man, from all I heard. Not many honest owners on the river these days." A bloodshot eye peered out at Slocum, as if challenging him to dispute that. Slocum wasn't going to mention anything about Jackson's smuggling scheme, whatever it might have been.

"You think I'm honest?" asked Slocum.

"Can't rightly say, one way or the other. You got the snap in your voice when it comes to giving commands, but you're not a river rat."

"I was an officer in the C.S.A.," said Slocum. "A captain."

"Being a captain's a different kettle of fish when you get off a horse and onto a boat," the man said. He came over and dropped into the chair in front of the desk. "Mind if I try one of the smokes? Been a while. All I been sucking into my gut is smoke off damned quirlies."

Slocum motioned for the man to take one of the thick, fragrant havanas. The man took the cigar and inhaled at its length, a look of supreme pleasure crossing his face. "Been a while," he said.

"You're sitting in my chair, sniffing my havana, getting ready to ask me for a light," said Slocum, "and you haven't told me either name or why you're here."

"Thanks for the fire," the man said as Slocum struck a lucifer and held it for him. "Why I'm here's as obvious as the nose on your face. And I'm Captain Sean O'Malley, best damn riverboat captain what ever steamed up or down the Mississippi."

"How long you been down on your luck?" asked Slocum.

O'Malley's bloodshot eye focused hard on Slocum. The man shifted in his chair and crossed his legs. He took several puffs on the cigar before answering.

"Long enough."

"Can't use a captain who spends all his time sucking at a bottle of Billy Taylor's finest whiskey. I may be a greenhorn when it comes to owning a riverboat, but I'm not so green I don't know how to choose good men to run the *Excalibur*."

"You inherited some real snakes," observed O'Malley.

"Might be true, but they haven't shown me anything bad enough for me to get rid of them. If Sam kept them on, they must be good enough to do their jobs right."

"You got a point. But Sam was a better owner than he was a captain."

"Mr. O'Malley, what are your credentials, other than spinning a good yarn?"

"Not much call for the skills I have, not these days what with all the damn Yankees running about." O'Malley reluctantly tossed the butt of his cigar into a tray on the desk, obviously considering asking Slocum for another. Instead he decided to tell about his life on the river.

"During the War I was a blockade runner. Since then there's not been that much call for me. The Yanks didn't take kindly to me working when it got out how I helped supply the Redlegs."

Slocum showed no emotion. This man had kept him alive during the War, and he hadn't even realized it. The blockade runners supplying Quantrill had taken risks that amazed even Slocum. For the most part, their heroism had gone unnoticed. But Slocum had noticed it at the time—and appreciated it still.

"You heard of the nasty business with the Redlegs, I see," said O'Malley. "I'm not proud those bastards were fighting on the same side as I was, but I'm damn proud of the fact I helped the Confederacy."

"After Grant took Vicksburg," said Slocum, "getting supplies was hard."

O'Malley read right what Slocum had said. "No wonder you're such a hard man. Running with them Redlegs kept a man tough as nails."

"I don't talk much about it," said Slocum. "If it's been such a long time since you captained a boat, what makes you think this one's right for you?"

"Some things you don't forget. The river's treacherous, she is. But the Hard Times Light and the Paddy Hen don't change. I can keep the pilots from screwing around there. And I run an honest boat when we're in port. Repairs are done for the lowest price I can get, and the damn repairs are going to be done right or I'll know the reason why."

Slocum nodded. He had been told that the pilot ran the riverboat once they entered the sluggish current of the river, but the captain had charge of any repairs and cargo problems while they were in port.

The crusty old man appealed to Slocum, even though his credentials for being captain on a boat as fine as the *Excalibur* were lacking. Slocum wondered if his decision wasn't influenced by O'Malley's claim to have been a blockade runner—but it didn't matter that much to Slocum.

"I'll pay you two hundred a month to get us to St. Louis. After that, things might change, including me as owner. Haven't decided yet."

"Two hundred!" bellowed O'Malley. The man leaped to

his feet and pounded a fist down on the mahogany desk. "You're a river pirate, that's what you are! Two hundred! I get four hundred or nothing!"

"Then it's nothing," said Slocum, "though I might be able to find a few dollars more. Since you're a former Confederate naval officer. Two-fifty."

"Three hundred, and you're getting a bargain for Sean O'Malley's fine services."

"Done," said Slocum. Three hundred a month was fair for an experienced captain. And, although Slocum didn't mention it, he needed someone aboard the riverboat who knew the ropes and who wasn't likely to be mixed up in whatever scheme it was that Sam had been involved in— and which had got him killed. "You make sure everything is ready for departure tomorrow morning. With the dawn."

"I know my job," said O'Malley, smiling proudly. "You don't have anything to worry about on that score. The *Excalibur*'s going to make the trip north in the best time this old lady's ever done."

A loud shriek from outside Slocum's office brought both of the men around. Slocum pulled out his pistol and rushed to see who was being killed aboard his riverboat.

3

Slocum rushed out of the captain's office and into the ball-room outside, Colt Navy in hand. He glanced down toward the stern of the boat and saw nothing. Without breaking stride he went in the other direction, dodging steamer trunks and cases left by stewards until the staterooms were assigned. Slocum burst out onto the elevated bandstand at the far end of the room just as another shriek echoed forth.

Slocum was positive he'd find Indians scalping half his crew. What he found brought him up short.

A portly woman stood in the middle of the dance floor, pointing and screaming. A slender young woman next to her tried to calm the matron. The harder she tried, the more the other woman shouted and carried on.

"What's wrong?" Slocum asked.

"Young man, this is a disgrace!" the fat woman declared. "Look at that! Look!"

"I don't see . . ." Slocum started. The rabbit-sized gray

wharf rat scuttled from its hiding place and darted across the floor. Without thinking, Slocum followed it and fired, his .31 caliber bullet finding its target. The rat tumbled forward and lay on the fine inlaid wood floor, kicking. Most men would have been dead. The rat refused to give up easily. A second shot killed it.

The woman let out another shriek that nearly deafened Slocum, then put the back of her hand to a wrinkled forehead and rocked back. "Oh, I feel so faint!"

The young woman made a valiant effort to keep the fat lady from crashing face forward to the floor. As it was, she only broke the fall.

"Steward!" bellowed Slocum. Two men in white linen jackets rushed into the ballroom. Slocum pointed to the rat. "Get rid of it."

"And her, sir?" asked one. "You want us to put her off, too?" The way he said it, nothing would have pleased him more. He smiled wickedly, his white teeth contrasting sharply with his black skin.

"Is there a doctor aboard who can look after her?"

"No, sir, not that I know of. But there is a notions peddler. Heard him saying he had some fine herb medicines. He might be of some service."

"Get him," Slocum said.

The steward went off to find the peddler.

"Mrs. Hortense, oh, please, Mrs. Hortense, don't be hurt." The young woman seemed genuinely concerned over the older woman's condition. Looking at her closely, Slocum was very interested in the young lady. Her long, lustrous brunette hair had been pulled back in a severe style intended to disguise her beauty but which highlighted the delicately boned face, the warm brown eyes, the lush, full red lips. She stroked over Mrs. Hortense's face, trying to revive the woman. From the way the fat woman's eyelids fluttered, Slocum guessed she was only putting on an act.

"There, there," he said soothingly, taking the young

woman's arm and pulling her to her feet. "We have someone coming to take a look at her."

"Mrs. Hortense is so delicate," the woman said earnestly. "The vapors take her when she's had a shock." She turned and looked at the tiny pool of blood where the rat had died. "This must have been too much for her, the sight of such an awful beast."

To Slocum, the fallen woman looked anything but delicate. He would hate to try to take her two falls out of three since she outweighed him by a goodly twenty pounds. But Slocum knew better than to say anything.

"Where's the fallen victim?" came a booming voice. "Ah, there the fair lady is. Oh, the horror of it!" the man cried dramatically. "But there is no need for worry now that I, James J. Poindexter, am here to rescue the fair damsel from her obvious bout with . . . distress."

The man knelt down, checked to be sure that he still held his audience, then reached into an inner pocket of his black cutaway coat and produced a clear glass bottle filled with a thick brown fluid.

"This, sirs and mademoiselle, is the latest discovery of science. It is none other than my Old Indian Root and Herb Remedy, the formula derived from tribal secrets passed down through the long centuries before the white man ever set foot on this fair continent. Not once in all that time has the Remedy failed to cure the afflicted."

He uncorked the bottle, sniffed delicately at the fumes rising from its mouth, and put it to Mrs. Hortense's lips. The woman sputtered and her eyes shot open.

"Th-that's awful," she spat out. "Take it away!"

"Another cure!" James J. Poindexter shot to his feet and struck a pose, holding the bottle aloft with one hand while his other held the lapel of his cutaway coat. "You have seen the Remedy work its magic anew on this delicate young lady. She revived! Though she was poised on the brink of death, the Remedy pulled her back safely. She—"

"Thanks," Slocum said, cutting off further sales pitch. "I'm certain Mrs. Hortense will testify to how good the Remedy worked. Later."

Poindexter went off, beaming at his success. The man's sharp eyes took in everything, however, and made Slocum feel uneasy about the peddler. Slocum bent down and helped the glaring woman to her feet.

"Are you all right?" Slocum asked.

"No, I am most assuredly am not!" Mrs. Hortense cried. "I demand to see the captain of this vessel instantly! I will lodge my complaint with him!"

Sean O'Malley weaved into the ballroom. Mrs. Hortense was in such a state that she didn't notice that the captain lacked a proper uniform or that he was already three sheets to the wind. But Slocum had to smile when O'Malley spoke. The timber of his voice proclaimed him captain.

"Madam, it has come to my attention that a great unpleasantness has been perpetrated on you. On behalf of the entire crew of the *Excalibur*, I offer my sincerest apologies." He bowed deeply, then reached out and took her pudgy hand, giving it a courtly kiss.

This seemed to pacify her. "Captain . . ."

"O'Malley, ma'am—Captain Sean O'Malley, at your personal service!"

"So gallant," she cooed. Turning to Slocum, she said, "I trust that the captain will fire you immediately. You are impudent and much too . . . too quick with that awful gun of yours!"

"Ma'am," spoke up Captain O'Malley, "rest assured that this will not happen again. John, there, was just doing his job, as he saw it. He meant no harm; to that I personally swear. Please come with me to my cabin. I have just taken aboard a most fine sherry. If I am not making too bold an overture, it would give me great pleasure if you would join me in a wee spot of it."

Mrs. Hortense made a face. "The medicine does require

some getting used to. A sip of sherry would help to alleviate the bitter taste."

O'Malley held out his arm. Mrs. Hortense took it, nose held high as she left the ballroom.

"Oh, I am so glad she didn't fire me," the young woman said, watching as the portly woman left.

"Fire you? Why?" Slocum was fascinated with the girl. She was still distraught over all that had happened, and her hurried breathing made her breasts rise and fall in a most fetching fashion. A slight flush colored her cheeks and heightened her beauty.

"Why, because of you shooting the rat, of course."

"You had nothing to do with that."

She shook her head. Some of her soft hair fell forward and haloed her face, turning her into an angel. Slocum started thinking about how long it had been since he'd seen a woman this pretty.

"You don't understand. Mrs. Hortense blames me for everything. I am her personal secretary and should be in control of these unfortunate events. I'm not. I'm afraid I am not very good at this at all."

"You handled it just fine, ma'am," Slocum said.

"Oh, see? I have forgotten my manners. Permit me to introduce myself, sir. I am Eleanore Dahlquist."

Slocum smiled and gave her his name.

"You're very good with your pistol, John."

"Better at it than I am at running a riverboat," he admitted ruefully.

"I'm afraid Mrs. Hortense will see you removed. She will soon have Captain O'Malley agreeing to just about anything. She can be very persuasive, you know."

Slocum smiled. Eleanore Dahlquist had much to learn. O'Malley had turned on the Irish charm to such an extent that Slocum hardly recognized the down-and-out riverboat captain. He guessed O'Malley had been one of the best—and that he'd handle Mrs. Hortense just fine.

"Mrs. Hortense might not be making the trip to St. Louis," said Slocum. Having the disagreeable woman on board the riverboat—*his* riverboat—wasn't the most exciting idea in the world.

Then Slocum looked again at Eleanore Dahlquist and decided that, if he had to take Mrs. Hortense to get Eleanore in the deal, it was a sacrifice he was inclined to make.

"She must," Eleanore said earnestly. "She must reach her husband immediately. We had been here on a visit to Mrs. Hortense's sick aunt. She received the telegram yesterday that Mr. Hortense is himself quite ill. We must return, and the *Excalibur* is the only ship leaving within the next few days."

"There's plenty of room aboard," said Slocum. "I'm sure we can fix you up with a cabin."

"Mrs. Hortense is very fussy," Eleanore said, wrinkling her nose in a way that pleased him. He smiled and ushered her toward one of the sumptuous sleeping rooms off the ballroom at the far end. Eleanore's soft brown eyes widened in awe when she saw the stateroom.

"This is gorgeous. Oh, I'd love to be able to afford a room like this." She walked around, lightly touching the satin spread on the brass bed, the delicate glass shades on the gaslight hung with lace, even the oil paintings nailed to the walls. Eleanore spun around, skirt lifting away from her ankles slightly and then dropped heavily onto the bed, enjoying the sensuous feel of the softness beneath her.

"You like it? You can have it."

"What?"

"If you like this," Slocum said, making a grand gesture, "then you must stay here." He liked the idea of the power owning the *Excalibur* gave him.

"Don't be ridiculous. Mrs. Hortense would never allow it. This stateroom must be expensive."

Slocum shrugged. "A hundred dollars upriver to St. Louis, I'd say. Maybe more."

"That settles it, then," Eleanore said firmly. "Mrs.

Hortense would never pay such a princely sum, and I certainly cannot afford it, not on the pittance she pays me."

"The owner insists," said Slocum, dropping onto the bed beside Eleanor. She was breathing harder again, breasts rising and falling under her tight bodice. Slocum reached out and put one hand alongside her cheek. Eleanore turned and kissed the palm of his hand.

"You don't have to do this. The rat didn't scare Mrs. Hortense that much. She was acting hateful, like she always does."

"I know that," said Slocum. Eleanore smiled weakly and started to stand.

He pulled her back down. Their eyes locked and said more than mere words ever could. Eleanore's lips parted slightly and her eyes closed. She tipped her head back slightly and waited. Slocum didn't hesitate. He moved forward, his lips brushing across the woman's. His arms circled her body and crushed her close, and then Eleanore surprised him. Slocum had thought she was a fragile little flower. The power in her embrace almost cracked his ribs, and the passion in her kiss bruised his lips.

"You're quite a hellion," Slocum told her.

"Then get on and ride, cowboy." Her lips kissed his ear, then her sharp teeth bit at the lobe. "Get in the saddle and break me!"

"First time a filly's ever asked for being rode," he said.

"This one wants it bareback!"

Her fingers fumbled for a moment, then tugged hard at Slocum's shirt. A couple of buttons tumbled off and went skittering across the floor to hide under the fancy carved armoire. Neither of them noticed. Slocum was too occupied working at the fastenings on Eleanore's simple dress. When he finally got it opened and pulled away from her sleek, milk-white body, he gasped.

"Those are about the prettiest sight I've seen," he said. Her breasts had been hidden by the tight bodice she wore. Eleanore was a full-bodied woman, ample in every dimension, and Slocum buried his face between these succulent mounds of flesh. Eleanore sighed and stroked his head as he licked and kissed and slowly spiralled up her left breast and found the coral button capping it.

"Oh, John!" Eleanore moaned. "More. Do that some more. I love the feel of your mouth sucking like that. Ummm!"

He began working his lips and tongue all over the hardened tip of her breast. Through the aroused nubbin he felt her heart triphammering wildly. She was as excited as he was—maybe more.

"Get your pants off," Eleanore said. "I enjoy this, but there's got to be more."

"Never meant to disappoint a lady," said Slocum, letting her work at his belt and trousers. He was finding himself more and more eager to get on with this. He had been riding trail for too long, and it had been a goodly spell since he'd been with a woman—and a damn sight longer since he'd been with one as pretty as Eleanore Dahlquist. And, Slocum had to admit honestly, still longer since he'd found one who knew her own mind and wanted what a man had to offer.

"Oh, John," she gasped. "You won't disappoint me with that." Slocum groaned when she took him in hand and began a gentle massaging. He felt the pressures mounting in his body and reluctantly pushed her away. He wasn't about to waste a good time just because it had been a while since he had bedded down with a woman.

Slocum kissed away her words and began moving his hands up and down her body, finding just the right places to touch, to stroke, to stimulate. Eleanore moaned incoherently now, lost in the throes of mounting passion. And Slocum wasn't about to let up, either. Both her breasts quivered with her every movement, and he treated them equally with his hot kisses and quick tonguings.

"Lower, John," the brunette gasped out. "I need you so. I do, I do!"

His mouth worked its way lower, to the slight dome of

her heaving belly. The fine hairs just below her navel tickled his nose. His tongue dipped briefly into the depression and then worked even lower. Eleanore sobbed and thrashed about constantly now.

"I need you in me, John. In, oh, dear God, yes, yes, in, in!" Eleanore's words were slurred with desire now. Slocum ran his fingers along the woman's inner thighs, stroking over the sleek, smooth flesh and feeling the effect this had on Eleanore. She gasped and sobbed out her needs.

Slocum worked his way back up her body, his chest crushing down atop the hard points of her nipples. Eleanore's slim, strong legs parted in wanton invitation. The man's hips worked forward; he touched the crinkly fur surrounding her most intimate territory. But Slocum had already explored here and knew where to go. He pushed forward, the tip of his cock slowing a bit when it detected the brunette's inner moistness, but only for an instant.

Sure of his carnal target, John Slocum swung his hips forward and buried himself to the hilt within the eager, clutching interior.

"You're so big," Eleanore said. "And it's been so long. So long since I felt this way about a man. So long since ... since ..."

"No need for talking," Slocum said. He felt sweat beading his entire body now. The hot tunnel he slid back and forth in crushed down on his hidden length, stroking and squeezing powerfully. He gasped and started moving faster. Eleanore's hips lifted off the bed, her legs circling his waist and her ankles locking behind his back.

They struggled together passionately, rising up in desire, cooling a mite, then surging upward again. Slocum felt the woman tense. A tiny trapped-animal gasp came from between her clenched teeth, and it felt like a soft, well-oiled mineshaft collapsing all around his pulsing manhood. Slocum didn't try to hold back then. He exploded, arms locked around the woman. They rolled over and over on the satin comforter, and came to rest side by side, spent.

"You're one hell of a woman," Slocum said, looking into her sweetly smiling face. Eleanore snuggled closer, her fingers restlessly roving up and down his back.

"Thank you," she said. "It's been so long."

"Didn't figure you were a virgin."

"I was married," she said. "My husband was killed in the War."

"You must have been married young. You're not more'n twenty now."

"Why, sir, you show all the manners of a Southern gentle-men. But I ought to have expected it from someone like you." Eleanore's fingers worked lower to the small of Slocum's back, and then drifted below that. Slocum thought he had died and gone straight to heaven.

"Your husband dying—is that why you're working as a secretary to that Mrs. Hortense?"

Eleanore nodded.

"Must be tiring work."

"I haven't worked for her all that long. Besides, she's not that bad," said Eleanore, "but she is very restrictive. She just thinks she knows what's best for me."

"*I* know what's best for you," said Slocum. "More of what we've been doing."

"Such a man," Eleanore said in mock surprise. She pushed him away and sat up in the bed, her breasts swaying in the most delightful manner possible. Slocum had a hard time getting his mind off them. Eleanore began dressing. "I shouldn't have left Mrs. Hortense for such a long time. She must be furious with me by now."

"Do you regret it, even if she is mad at you?"

"Quit fishing for compliments, sir," Eleanor said brightly. "You were just fine, thank you." She bent and kissed him, then went back to dressing. "Of course I don't mind. But I will have to get her settled in her cabin."

"Captain O'Malley will probably see to it that she's put in one across the ballroom."

"I should be near her. That *is* my job."

"I was serious about you staying in this room. Unless you don't like it."

"I love it. The only one sure to be finer is the owner's cabin."

"Would you prefer to stay there?"

"John, what are you saying? You'll be the one getting fired if the owner finds out what you're offering me. Why, he might fire you if he finds out what we've been doing in this lovely stateroom."

Slocum lounged back and smiled. He was liking this more and more. Being the owner of a riverboat had definite benefits he hadn't thought about.

"The owner's a good friend of mine," he said. "He'll go along with anything I say."

Eleanore Dahlquist straightened imaginary wrinkles in her dress, turning one way and then the other in front of the full-length mirror mounted on the wall. When she was satisfied, she patted her hair into some semblance of order.

"John, you have the wildest imagination. Just bringing me here was quite dangerous for both of us. I don't want to even think of what might happen if the owner caught us. You probably don't even know the owner by sight."

"I'm the owner," he said, enjoying the brunette's reaction. Yes, indeed, he was going to enjoy this trip to St. Louis as owner of the *Excalibur*. While he was sorry Sam Jackson had died, there was nothing he could do about that. Why not enjoy this windfall to the hilt?

"And here I was thinking I wasn't going to enjoy going up the smelly old river," said Eleanore. The brunette looked around the stateroom, her eyes wide at the realization she could stay here. She flashed him a white smile, blew him a kiss, and quickly left the stateroom. Slocum stretched, feeling better than he had in months.

He dressed and went to see how Sean O'Malley had fared with Mrs. Hortense.

4

Slocum stopped by the bandstand where the brass band was supposed to play in the ballroom and watched as Captain O'Malley guided Mrs. Hortense to a cabin, Eleanore Dahlquist trailing behind like an obedient puppy dog. But Slocum saw the expression on the brunette's face and the slow, lewd wink she gave him when she noticed him. Slocum smiled in return as the trio vanished into the stateroom. He continued his own exploration of the *Excalibur*, seeing that O'Malley had already moved into the captain's cabin and taken it over for his own.

One by one, Slocum checked out the other rooms along the perimeter of the ballroom. Each seemed to be grander than the last, but one in particular struck Slocum's fancy. If he was going to play owner all the way up the river to St. Louis, he might as well go in style. He stood in the doorway of a room that was everything he had ever dreamed of seeing.

Oil paintings decorated the walls, a fancy green deep pile rug stretched over the floor, and a brass bed even larger than the one in the cabin where he had made love to Eleanore dominated the center of the room. The gilt trim all over the room had been cleaned recently, and there was a cool serenity about the room that soothed Slocum. He had been through so much that he needed the sanctuary this room offered.

He signalled a passing steward and said, "This is my new cabin. Make sure Captain O'Malley is comfortable in his, then see to mine."

"Yes, sir," the steward said. "Will you be wantin' your meals served in the room, or will you take them with the passengers?"

Slocum thought of eating with Mrs. Hortense and inwardly detested the idea, but with her came Eleanore.

"With the others," he said. "No need putting you out any."

"No problem, sir."

"Where's Leander Martin likely to be this time of day?" he asked. "I want him to show me around."

"Mr. Martin, sir?" the steward asked, eyes widening in surprise. "He's like to be down lookin' over the cargo. That's about all he ever do."

Slocum looked shrewdly at the steward. "Why don't you like him? He do something to you?"

"No, sir, not like some of the white folks who ship on as passengers. It's just that he's a difficult man to get along with when he's in one of those moods."

Slocum said, "Doesn't much matter to me what mood he's in. I owe it to Sam's memory to do what I can to keep the *Excalibur* running smoothly." Slocum saw the expression on the steward's face. Many questions would be whispered about what had happened to Sam Jackson, and even more rumors would fly. Slocum added, "Sam was a friend of mine. It had been a long time since I'd seen him, but he was a good man."

The steward nodded and went about his work without another word. A cold, sinking feeling worked its way up from the soles of Slocum's feet and stopped in the pit of his stomach. He was an outsider on the *Excalibur* and would be the butt of jokes and rumors. Most of the crew would think the worst of him whenever Sam's name came up.

He went to the end of the ballroom and out onto the deck walkway outside. There were twenty cabins inboard able to hold as many as fifty passengers, but the walkway looked down to the cargo deck where another two hundred or more passengers might stay for short trips. The major portion of the cargo had been loaded, and already some deck passengers lounged on bales of cotton and tobacco. Slocum saw one man pull a leaf of tobacco from a bale, roll it up, and begin to chew on it. Even uncured, the flavor and appeal of the tobacco drew users.

"Martin," Slocum called out, seeing the *Excalibur*'s chief clerk below. "I want a word with you."

Martin either didn't hear or ignored him. Before Slocum could shout down again, Martin vanished into the cargo hold. His anger mounting, Slocum went around to the stairs and hurried down to the deck passenger area. All the roustabouts averted their eyes and stared down at the crates and bales in front of them; all banter stopped between them. All Slocum heard was a doleful voice singing from the stern:

"Way down on the Ohio
  We wander alone.
  We is drunk as the devil,
  Oh, let us alone."

Slocum turned toward the man singing, found a convenient crate, and perched on it. Slocum felt as if they drifted along in a bubble, just him and the roustabout. The rest of the crew moved to exile them.

The roustabout finally noticed, stopped singing, and looked up from the hawser he coiled.

"There's no need to stop," said Slocum.

"Sorry, suh. Didn't mean to be slackin' off on the job." The man went back to untangling and coiling the rope.

"I meant your singing."

"Only sings when I is happy."

"I make you unhappy?" asked Slocum.

The man turned. Dark eyes bored into Slocum's green ones, then dropped to the pistol Slocum carried in the cross-draw holster. The well-worn ebony grip and the obvious hard use the gun itself had been put to. The whipcord hardness of Slocum's body. The cold eyes.

"It's bein' said you done killed Cap'n Sam."

"It's a lie. Two men came up and shotgunned him in cold blood." Slocum's hand instinctively went to the shallow groove cut alongside his head. He pulled back when the pain told him not to touch.

"You killed men before. I read it in your eyes."

"I fought in the War," Slocum said, his mind touching on all the times he had crouched atop a hill, squinting for the glint of sunlight against Yankee braid. Kill the officers, kill the enemies' will to fight. He'd shot down more bluecoat officers than he cared to remember, but remember them he did. Each and every one. At times like this, in his darkest nightmares, he remembered.

"Somethin's botherin' you bad," said the roustabout. "And I don't think it's guilt about shootin' down Cap'n Sam. You didn't do it, did you?"

Slocum shook his head. "We all carry things in our head we'd as soon not. Sam's death isn't something I'm going to forget—and it's not going unavenged. I'll find out who's responsible and do what's necessary."

"Sure am glad I don't have nothin' to do with it, no, suh. You's not the one to have mad at me."

Slocum laughed at that. "Tell me what you can about the *Excalibur*. If I'm to get it up the river to St. Louis, I need to find out what's necessary and what isn't."

"Man, you surely are new to the river," said the roustabout. "The owner don't do nothin' on most boats 'cept sit back with his feet high up on a desk and brag to all the womenfolks 'bout how important he is. The cap'n's responsible for the boat when we're docked, and the pilot stands way up there on the texas deck like he was some newfangled god when we's on the river."

"The captain has nothing to do with the boat when we're actually steaming?"

The roustabout shook his head.

Slocum let out a lungful of air. No wonder Sean O'Malley had been so surprised at the way he had spoken to the red-haired pilot Henry Sanders.

"A good cap'n keeps his eye on all that happens, but he don't meddle none with the pilot. They's cranky sons of bitches, the pilots."

"We've been talking, and we still aren't introduced," Slocum said. He gave his name, then stuck out his hand. For a moment, the roustabout was taken aback.

"Ras, they calls me Ras." He shook Slocum's hand as if it would turn into a snake and bite him.

"What's that short for?"

"You listen up good. You hear more'n what's bein' said. The full name's Erasmus Washington. I been workin' on the *Excalibur* for well nigh two years. Cap'n Sam was the best on the river, bar none. I'm gonna miss him."

Slocum slapped Washington on the shoulder and stood. He heard the click of a hammer being pulled back, and this saved him. Slocum was already falling forward when the sharp, harsh pistol crack sounded. The bullet ripped a new gouge just a fraction of an inch above the groove cut by the buckshot that had killed Jackson. Pain welled up in Slocum's head, red and confusing. He pushed himself off the slippery deck and then sank back down when a wave of dizziness hit him. Slocum heard Ras Washington bellowing, and the pounding of feet followed by rough hands pulling him to a sitting position. He winced and touched the red stream pouring down the side of his head.

"You all right, Mr. Slocum?"

Slocum forced himself to focus on the roustabout. His eyes kept wandering. Hands shook him, and the pain wiped out all the shock. Slocum croaked out that he was.

"Who tried to backshoot Mr. Slocum?" Washington demanded. "Who do that to him?"

Slocum pushed to his feet and looked around at the tight knot of crew. "Where's Martin?" he asked, strength returning slowly.

"He ain't around. Nobody's seen Mr. Martin," came the quick answer from the middle of the crowd.

Someone else spoke up, saying cautiously, "Saw him in the cargo hold a few minutes ago."

"Get him. Now!"

Slocum wasn't in any mood to argue. His words carried the sharp edge of command. Boots shuffled on the deck, and in a few seconds only Erasmus Washington and Slocum stood on the stern.

"Here he is," said Washington.

Leander Martin glared down at Slocum from atop a stack of crates, as if accusing him of some crime. Slocum returned the gaze unflinchingly. He was madder than a wet hen by now. Sam Jackson had been killed, and now someone was trying to do the same to him. Slocum wanted answers.

"Get down here," he snapped.

Martin dropped to the deck and defiantly stood, legs spread, hands clenched into fists and balanced on his hips. "What kind of damn fool mess have you got yourself into, *sir?*" The sneer made Martin's lip curl like a flag flapping in the wind.

"You're the one in charge of everything going on. Did you see who shot at me?"

"The captain's in command of a riverboat when it's docked. Why don't you ask him?"

Slocum didn't see any telltale bulge a gun would make under Martin's shirt, but this didn't mean the man couldn't have taken the potshot at Slocum and then stashed the gun in a convenient spot, planning to retrieve it later.

"There's no reason for us to like one another," said Slocum, "but if I find out if was you who shot at me just now, I'm going to throw a line around your feet, dump you overboard, and pull you all the way to St. Louis. Do I make myself clear?"

Slocum waited for Martin's anger to reach the boiling point. When it did, the chief clerk would curse and carry on and then quit, storming off the *Excalibur* in a fit of wrath.

It didn't happen. And this made Slocum even more suspicious. River men were proud, and there was always another sternwheeler coming along looking for able-bodied crew. Leander Martin had no reason to stay aboard a ship if the owner blamed him for something he hadn't done.

"I'll try to keep what you said in mind, sir." The surliness intensified rather than going away. Martin spun and vanished amid the jungle of bales on the deck.

"You sure made yourself a powerful enemy in Mr. Martin," observed Washington. "If you don't mind my sayin' so."

"He wants to stay close to the *Excalibur* for some reason," said Slocum. "I want to find out why."

"You thinkin' he maybe had something to do with Cap'n Sam's killing?"

Slocum ignored the question and asked, "Who can show me the engines and boilers? I understand they're made by Hippel and Evans of Albany, Indiana."

"You do learn quick," said Washington, smiling. "You get that off some paper to impress the chief engineer?"

Slocum laughed. "Sam mentioned it, bragging on the engines. It just stuck in my mind."

"You'll get along all right with Mr. Macallum."

Slocum had glanced at the crew roster and identified the man with the engineering crew.

Washington confirmed this, adding, "He be the best damn engineer up or down the river. I do declare he can squeeze

more steam out of a log than any man I ever did see, livin'
or dead."

"High praise." Slocum went to find the engineer and see
if the engines were in as good a condition as Sam Jackson
had boasted. As he went, Slocum kept a wary eye out for
any further trouble. Out on the prairie a man might be
bushwhacked, and the buzzards would dine on his bones.
That wasn't a pretty way to cash in your chips, but Slocum
accepted it. On the river it was entirely different.

A man might slide into those churning mud-yellow waters
and never be seen again. Becoming fish food made him a
sight uneasier than the thought of vultures picking his skel-
eton clean. Slocum couldn't say why, since dead was dead,
but he vowed to avoid that particular fate. Slocum walked
just a bit closer to cargo stacked on the deck until he came
to the oilers laboring to get the *Excalibur*'s engines into top
form.

"You be the new owner, eh?" asked a boisterous man,
coming up and slapping Slocum on the back. "You can trust
old Macallum with these wee bairns." The man actually
patted one of the thirty-two-foot-long boilers as if it were
flesh and blood and might respond to his affection.

"Looks as if you're keeping everything in good shape,"
said Slocum.

"Aye, that I am. Fine engines, just fine. Cap'n Jackson
knew how to buy the best, he did. Sad about him, sad,
indeed." Slocum got the idea that Macallum didn't care who
owned or commanded the *Excalibur* as long as he personally
could fondle the engines.

"I'm not looking for any trouble on this run," said Slocum,
"but trouble is finding me. Just wanted to make sure there
wouldn't be any problems once we start up tomorrow."

"Great engines," the engineer said. "We got the eight
boilers all cleared of scale, every inch of that eleven-foot
stroke is greased to perfection, and I got two assistants inside
working on the engines themselves."

"Inside?"

"There're three-foot cylinders on the engines what need tending to," Macallum said, as if Slocum were the stupidest man alive. He turned and shook his head as he went back to work. The massive steam engines were more interesting to him than any owner.

Slocum started back up toward his cabin, finding the stairs and beginning the climb. But he stopped halfway up and looked back onto the cargo deck. The roustabouts stood clustered together, whispering.

"Anything the matter?" Slocum asked, pitching his voice so that it carried the sharpness of command. He had seen behavior like this before, and he tried not to let his uneasiness over it become too apparent. Just after he had been promoted to corporal of sharpshooters in Jackson's Brigade, there had been a small insurrection. The men had been dissatisfied with the wormy food and the long hours walking, only to fight halfway into the night and then do it all over again the next day. A few of them had got together, expressions just like those he read on these men's faces, and had decided to demand their rights.

They'd rioted, and half of them had been cut down. Slocum's mouth went a bit dry when he remembered the order his lieutenant had given. He had shot down four of the mutineers —men he had eaten with, fought with, laughed and cried with. The order had been a necessary one, but it hadn't made the killing any easier for Slocum.

These roustabouts smouldered inside with the same unfocused anger. They wanted to strike out but they couldn't rightly figure out at what.

"If you're done socializing, get back to work," he told them.

"We want to talk to the captain," said one man.

"Whoever the old sot is," muttered another.

"Captain O'Malley will be down to talk with you soon enough," Slocum said. If O'Malley were half the man Slocum thought he was, in spite of the alcohol burning in his veins, he would be able to get control of the crew. Slocum knew better than to do more than promise the crew this much; he was an outsider, a man who had taken their owner–captain's place under mysterious circumstances. Let a river man tend to their problems and they might go away. If Slocum so much as tried to give them a command, he'd be swimming in the muddy river, fighting for his life.

Slocum turned and felt their hot, angry eyes burning into his back. He heard a clank of metal against the wood decking and Washington's low voice cursing at someone. Slocum didn't have to see what had happened to know how close he had been to getting knifed in the back. Erasmus Washington had saved him that fate—this time.

Still, one agitated sailor meant nothing. His passion had flared at the wrong instant. What worried Slocum was the backshooter. That meant someone with a motive for murder who wouldn't vanish with a few swigs from a corn-liquor jug and the chance to tell tale tales with his friends.

Above him he heard the scuffle of feet and the muted sounds of an argument. Slocum took the steps two at a time and, just as he reached the passenger deck, heard the sharp report of a pistol. He froze, thinking his unseen assailant had again tried to kill him, but no bullet raced by him. Slocum felt like a fool running his fingers over his belly checking for a wound that wasn't there.

Slocum looked up in time to see a brightly colored object falling from the texas deck past the passenger walkway. The heavy thud of a body hitting the cargo deck told him whoever that had been was dead.

He ran to the railing and peered over. The roustabouts gathered around the twisted, gracelessly sprawling body of Henry Sanders.

The pilot was obviously dead.

5

Slocum's hand rested on the ebony handle of his Colt, but he didn't draw. There was no clear target and, unless he missed his bet by a mile, whoever had killed Henry Sanders was long gone. Not off the *Excalibur,* perhaps, but certainly not standing around waiting for someone to find him with a smoking pistol in his hand.

Or *her* hand, Slocum had to admit. Anyone who peacocked around like Sanders had to attract the women. Lots of them. A jealous husband, a jilted lover; any number of people might want Sanders dead.

Slocum didn't believe that for a minute.

Cautiously, he went up the stairs leading to the pilot house and the texas deck in front of it. At the top of the stairs he saw half a dozen men leaning over the edge, looking down to where the corpse lay on the cargo deck. They turned when they heard Slocum approaching.

"You see that, Mr. Slocum?" asked one of the younger men. "That stupid son of a bitch upped and fell over the edge. Walked right off, he did. I saw it!"

Slocum frowned. All the river men carried pistols stuck in their belts, and from the way they clustered together, the group wouldn't take kindly to him asking to inspect each pistol.

"Just what did you see?" Slocum asked.

"Why, just as I said. Mr. Sanders was forward checking the currents so's he'd know how to handle them tomorrow morning. He just swung around, surprised like, threw his arms up into the air like he was cheering in last year's Mardi Gras parade, and stepped right off." The youth chuckled. "He looked like a goddamn gooney bird trying to fly, his arms flapping and his mouth suckin' wind."

"He was shot," said Slocum.

The men quieted and looked from one to the other, then back at Slocum. "You accusin' us, Mr. Owner?" drawled one. His fingers tapped lightly on the butt of the decrepit cap and ball pistol shoved into his belt. It wouldn't take much before the river man decided to see how big a hole his old pistol might put in Slocum's gut.

"I wasn't saying any of you did it," Slocum explained, keeping his voice level. "There was more to it than you saw. Any of you hear a gunshot before Sanders went over the deck edge?"

Six heads shook.

Slocum went to the verge and peered down. An instant of vertigo passed. The roustabouts had already taken care of Sanders's body. Slocum didn't have to ask if they had notified the marshal. That would be the last thing any river man considered. Sanders was one of their own, and they'd handle it. Just as Sam Jackson would be taken care of, when the proper time came.

Slocum pushed back through and down to the ballroom searching for Sean O'Malley. He found the captain sitting behind the huge mahogany desk, poring over a stack of papers. The man continually licked his lips and his hands shook, but some of the haggard look had gone.

"Slocum? Been going over the manifests. Terrible choices made by this Jackson fellow. The rates are way too low to make a good profit. We're not running a charity ship. The *Excalibur* will show a nice gain if we up the passenger rates from three cents a mile to four. What do they care? The stage costs them six cents, and we give them a comfortable place to park their fat asses."

"Captain," Slocum said, raising his voice to get O'Malley's attention, "someone just murdered the pilot."

"How's that again?"

"Sanders was shot in front of the pilot house and fell to the cargo deck. We have to get another pilot if we want to leave."

"Talked with the boy. An arrogant horse's ass, he was, but he convinced me he knew the river. Replacing him ain't going to be easy, not this late in the game."

"Find someone," said Slocum.

"You're the owner."

"I hired you. One rotten decision a day is all I want to make."

O'Malley laughed. "In spite of that hard stare of yours, Slocum, I'm comin' to like you. And it was no mistake makin' me the captain of this fine riverboat."

Slocum looked at the papers strewn about the desk and decided O'Malley was the one for the job. A small, crabbed set of notes rested to one side, showing O'Malley had worked through the intricate books left by Sam Jackson and had come to solid conclusions.

"Anything wrong about the cargo?" Slocum asked.

"Wrong? How do you mean?"

"Is there anything being carried that's out of the ordinary?"

The question made O'Malley scratch his stubbled chin. The captain finally shook his head. "Nothing worth mentioning. Are you telling me there might be something worth killing for hidden away in this?" He tapped the manifest.

"Sam's dead, I've been shot twice, and now Sanders is

dead. Someone's trying to get the message across that the *Excalibur* is dangerous to be on."

"That why you're still leaking blood down the side of your head?"

Slocum touched the sluggish flow. The recent bullet wound had opened again. He dabbed at it with a rag O'Malley shoved across the desk. Slocum tried not to think about how dirty the cloth was or what O'Malley had been doing with it.

"You're going to have some trouble with the crew," Slocum told the captain. "They've been muttering, and not a one of them will look me in the eye. Can't say what this might mean on a riverboat, but in the army it meant trouble."

"Means mutiny here, too," O'Malley said. "Seen it enough times to be scared spitless." Slocum didn't think O'Malley sounded in the least frightened of the prospect of mutiny. If anything, the man's rheumy eyes began to sharpen and glow with the challenge.

"During the War," O'Malley went on, talking more to himself than to Slocum now, "I had to deal with mutinies all the time. Never enough food, the Yank gunboats threatening us at every turn of the river, and pay? Never! We got rumpled slips of paper from the Confederacy. Damn IOU's!"

"Better quit moving the papers from one stack to the other and get to looking for a new pilot. I didn't much care for Sanders, but from all accounts he was a good pilot. Replacing him might be hard," Slocum said.

"That it will be," said O'Malley. "I talked with the second pilot. A bright enough lad, but inexperienced. He's only been full pilot for two trips up and down the river. Not enough to know how tricky the Mississippi can be. Smithson's his name."

"You don't think we can make the trip with just the one pilot?"

O'Malley snorted in contempt. "Hell, son, it's bad enough with two of the sons of bitches to stand watch. They do back-to-back shifts the whole way, four hours on and four off. Don't ever take the risk of having a sleepy or drunk pilot in the wheelhouse. That'll sink a boat faster'n anything I know."

"You're the captain," said Slocum.

"That I am," O'Malley said with some satisfaction.

"I'm going into the city to clear up some business," Slocum told the man. "How do I go about getting some spending money out of the *Excalibur's* account?"

O'Malley cocked his head to one side and peered at Slocum. "You're not about to go gallivantin' off, never to be seen again, are you?"

The idea had occurred to Slocum. Along with the *Excalibur,* he had inherited Sam Jackson's enemies. Worst of all, Slocum had no inkling who they might be. He had to watch his every step, duck at every sudden noise, draw down on every shadow. This wasn't a life he enjoyed leading, but then it wasn't much different from what he'd gone through the past few years. Judge killers never rested easy.

Still, Slocum felt some obligation to Sam's memory. The man had been a friend. They'd drifted out of touch during the War, but Sam was still a friend. Slocum had no need for a riverboat like the *Excalibur* and had only been given it because no one else was around when Sam was bleeding to death. The *Excalibur* belonged to Marie Jackson up in St. Louis, and Slocum intended for her to get it.

"I'm staying aboard till we get to St. Louis," Slocum explained. "Then you'll have a new owner for the boat: Mrs. Jackson."

"First I heard that there was one, but then I never knew Jackson, 'cept by reputation."

"I'll be back. Can you lend me as much as fifty dollars, gold?"

"Lend you?" said O'Malley, eyes widening in surprise. "You're the owner, son. You can take what you want. Don't much matter what I think, one way or the other."

"This is all new to me," said Slocum.

"I think you'd better get a doctor to look at that head

wound of yours—both wounds. Your brains are rattlin' around inside so much they'll keep the passengers awake if we hit any rough water.

O'Malley fumbled in a green tin box and pulled out two double eagles and a handful of small-denomination greenbacks. "This'll have to do you," he said, counting out ten of the bills and pushing them and the coins across to Slocum. "Now get out of here and let me get to hirin' a new pilot."

Slocum wobbled a bit as he walked. He stopped in front of the stateroom door and braced himself until the dizziness passed. He looked up to see Eleanore Dahlquist staring at him, concern in her soft brown eyes.

"Are you all right, John? You're so pale." She let out a tiny gasp when she saw the bloody groove on the side of his head. "That's awful! Get inside and let me fix you up."

Slocum went into his stateroom and collapsed onto the bed. He was barely aware of Eleanore's gentle fingers moving over the bullet crease or her saying, "There doesn't seem to be any other damage. Saw a man once hit in the head whose eyes wouldn't focus right. He died. But you look to be in good enough condition to tell me what happened."

Slocum told the brunette all that had gone on, then told her, "I'm going into town. Would you care to join me?"

"Oh, John, I can't. Mrs. Hortense might need me." Eleanore looked stricken at the idea of passing up a last tour through New Orleans. Slocum knew she hadn't had much chance to see the city due to nursemaiding Mrs. Hortense around.

"Won't be gone long," he coaxed.

"She'll be livid," said Eleanore, but the decision had been made. "I'll be back in a second. Let me get my bonnet!"

Slocum changed his shirt and tossed the bloodied one onto the bed. Let the steward tend to it. Slocum had to smile. He could get used to being waited on hand and foot. Owning the *Excalibur* had definite advantages.

Disadvantages, too, he remembered. The need to replace

a pilot, the unrest among the crew, someone trying to gun him down. All this, Slocum decided, offset any real gain. Besides, he thought of himself as nothing more than a caretaker getting the *Excalibur* north to St. Louis and Mrs. Jackson. By rights, Sam had meant the riverboat to be turned over to his wife, but fate had decreed differently.

"Ready, John?" asked Eleanore. She spoke softly, almost timidly.

"Ready as I'll ever be, he said, cinching up his gunbelt a notch so that the Colt rode a bit higher on his left hip. "I want to take care of my horse and tack."

Together they went down the gangplank. Slocum felt the eyes of the roustabouts fixed on him, burning hot holes in his back. He didn't turn around even though icicles ran up and down his spine, as he waited for another bullet to come hunting for him. He relaxed by the time they reached Canal Street. He pointed up Julia Street, then hailed a carriage.

"No sense walking when we can ride in style," he told Eleanore.

"Mrs. Hortense always insists on a carriage," Eleanore said, not understanding Slocum. The man again saw the difference between those who had money—or, like Eleanore, those who lived in the shadow of money—and poor dirt farmers like himself, who thought of riding in a rented carriage as an absurdly expensive luxury. If he didn't ride on a horse, he walked around a town. Somehow, even though he had come by a riverboat worth thousands of dollars, Slocum had trouble spending even a tiny portion of that wealth. When a nickel was all he was used to carrying in his pocket, spending a dime for a carriage struck him as opulent, no matter that he had taken fifty dollars from the boat's petty-cash box.

"Are you taking your horse on board?" Eleanore asked.

"Selling her. Saddle and bridle, too. I reckon I can get better when I reach St. Louis." He told the woman to wait while he went into the stable and dickered with the owner. After subtracting the fifty cents a day for boarding the horse,

Slocum pocketed twenty dollars. Horse and saddle had been worth more, but not much more.

Rejoining Eleanore, he asked, "Food? Even though I had a big meal this morning, everything that's happened has given me a powerful appetite."

"Oh, John, could we eat at one of those French places? The ones with the lace tablecloths and the fancy bone china?"

The driver started off through the tangle of New Orleans streets and delivered them in front of a restaurant Slocum would never have picked in a hundred years.

"It looks so expensive," Eleanore said, obviously starting to change her mind.

"I owe it to you," he said. "You bandaged me up as good as any doctor could have done." Slocum decided he might as well learn to spend some of his money. So what if a meal at this fancy French restaurant cost five dollars? He had it, and more.

The maitre d' looked down his nose at them as they entered, but said nothing as he led Slocum and Eleanore to an isolated table in the rear. Slocum started to demand one by a window, then stopped. While the maitre d' was being insulting in his placement, and Slocum knew it, Slocum didn't want to be too conspicuous. He still had federal marshals on his trail.

And the two men who'd killed Sam Jackson wouldn't think twice about shooting him through a window while he ate fancy French food.

"This is so . . . cozy," Eleanore murmured. That made Slocum feel better about not demanding another table. It *was* nice here in the back of the restaurant.

The waiter came and he, too, looked as if he had gas pains even speaking to Slocum, but the expression faded when it became apparent Slocum was no mere drifter. He might not often eat in posh restaurants, but he was no green-horn at this, either. His travels had brought him into contact with enough men with varied skills. One of them had claimed to be a cordon bleu chef trained in Paris. Slocum never knew if Frenchy lied through his teeth or not, but the man fixed up more than a plate of beans every night for the men in the sniper company. Slocum had listened and remembered most of what the cook had said.

It impressed Eleanore and made Slocum feel worlds better than he had for a long time. The lovely woman was such a delectable combination of demure good looks and fiery passion. He'd settle for demure now if he got another crack at the unleashed desires later.

"You're a man with many talents, John," she said. "Even though I've been with Mrs. Hortense and seen what she does, it's strange for me to try ordering in such a place. Why, the menu wasn't even in English!"

Slocum started to tell her about Frenchy and the bragging he had done when a tall man dressed in an elegant pearl-gray morning coat with black velvet tab collars came and stood beside him. The man cleared his throat and placed one hand on his lapel, as if getting ready to give an oration.

Slocum looked up, saying nothing.

"Mr. Slocum?" the man asked. His voice was deep, resonant, cultured. Everything about him reeked of money.

"Don't believe I know you," Slocum said, not willing to admit to anything. The memory of marshals on his trail haunted him, awake or asleep.

"My name is Berton Fellows, of Fellows, Abercrombie and Lynch." The way he said it told Slocum that he was expected to recognize the names, but he had no clue as to who they were supposed to be.

Eleanore came to his rescue. "You're a partner in the biggest law firm in New Orleans?" she asked.

"Ma'am," Fellows said, bowing slightly in her direction. "I do have that honor and privilege."

"Don't think either of us needs a lawyer," said Slocum.

"I am sorry, Mr. Slocum. Please excuse me. It is not what I can do for you, but rather the other way around. You see, I have a client who is very interested in purchasing the *Excalibur*. I understand that you are the new owner."

"Word travels fast," muttered Slocum.

"Indeed," said Fellows in a dry tone. "Mr. Jackson dealt with another law firm, but you are well aware of that, I am sure."

Slocum wasn't, but he said nothing. The less he spoke, the less he showed how ignorant he was of Sam's business dealings and running a riverboat.

Fellows continued, "The *Excalibur* is one of the finer boats on the river. My client, who prefers to remain unnamed until an agreement has been reached, is willing to make a very generous offer."

Slocum looked at Eleanore, then back to Fellows. "How generous?" he asked.

"Eighteen thousand dollars," said Fellows. "This is as much profit as the *Excalibur* is likely to turn in three fine years of service or five years of good luck. I realize you are not a river man born and bred. This offer certainly allows you to, say, purchase a farm or a ranch. Raising horses for stud might appeal to you more than moving cotton bales up and down the Mississippi."

"Eighteen thousand?" said Eleanore, stunned by the huge amount.

"I may legally own the riverboat," said Slocum, "but I think of myself more as a caretaker. Maybe trustee is the right word. I intend taking the *Excalibur* to St. Louis and turning it over to Sam Jackson's widow. The boat's not mine. Maybe legally it is, but not morally."

"There are other arrangements that might be made," said Fellows, suavely shifting to another tack. "Mrs. Jackson can be sent the money from the sale—and you, Mr. Slocum, would surely be entitled to an agent's fee. Ten percent, perhaps?"

"You're offering me eighteen hundred dollars, and you'll still pay Marie Jackson the full purchase price?"

"That seems fair. Don't you agree, Mr. Slocum? Ma'am?" Slocum saw that Berton Fellows worked his wiles on Eleanore as well as on him.

"John, it is a great deal of money. And Mrs. Jackson would only sell the boat herself. She probably wasn't interested in the *Excalibur*. You'd be doing her a favor."

Slocum shook his head. "I can't decide for her. While this is a generous offer, I think I'll deliver the *Excalibur* and let Mrs. Jackson figure out what to do with the riverboat in St. Louis."

"Is it only a matter of price? If so, we can negotiate."

"No."

Fellows saw that Slocum wanted only to return to his meal with Eleanore. He cleared his throat for one last try. "I have not been entirely frank with you, Mr. Slocum. While the riverboat is a fine specimen, what my client is really in desperate need of is a cargo."

"What?" Slocum could not understand what the high-priced lawyer meant.

"The cane and...uh...tobacco and cotton. My client would like to purchase it all. At the same price you'd get in St. Louis. You can have the profit for the trip without ever leaving the dock."

"That's the most cockamamie thing I've ever heard," said Slocum. "Cargoes are sitting on the docks rotting for lack of transport to the North. What is so special about the cargo aboard the *Excalibur* that you'd be willing to buy the whole damned riverboat to get it?"

"My client is a bit eccentric. When you have a great deal of money, it is possible to indulge yourself in whims. Consider this a rich man's whim, Mr. Slocum."

"I won't consider it at all. The cargo has been contracted for. Sam wanted it delivered to St. Louis, and I am only doing what he had obligated himself to do. The *Excalibur* belongs to Mrs. Jackson, in principle if not legal fact at the moment, and the freight already loaded will be delivered on schedule—to St. Louis. Good day, Mr. Fellows."

Slocum watched the lawyer from the corner of his eye. The stricken expression on the man's face told the story. He had expected the stupid trail hand to jump at the offer of such a huge amount of money. Slocum doubted Berton Fellows had dealt with very many men who had a sense of duty.

Slocum couldn't think of himself as rich. He was only caretaker for the *Excalibur*. But he had something better than all the gold in the world. He had his honor.

"John, was that the right thing to do? He offered so much money!" Eleanore shook her head in wonder.

"That's what makes it right. No one just walks over and offers that kind of money to a stranger unless there's a lot more tied up in the deal."

"But what?"

Slocum didn't answer. Whatever it was, Sam Jackson had been killed for it. And Slocum now knew for a fact it was aboard the *Excalibur*.

"Finish your meal," he said. "I want to return to the boat as soon as possible. I have to buy some new clothes and then we'll go back."

"Clothes?" Eleanore said, her eyes shining. "Could I do just a bit of shopping, John? This is such a fine city, and I didn't get to see any of it. I was only here two days before Mrs. Hortense hired me, and since then there's been no time to do a thing."

Even though Slocum was in a hurry to return to the *Excalibur* he couldn't deny Eleanore her bit of shopping.

"A little," he allowed. "But not for too long."

"Oh, no!" she promised. "I'll be quick as a rabbit about my shopping." Content, the brunette returned to her meal, licking her lips with real enjoyment at the end.

Slocum attacked the remaining portion of his frog legs with a vengeance and soon reduced them to gnawed bones. Slocum paid the hefty bill and left with Eleanore Dahlquist on his arm, aware of the cool stare given him by Berton Fellows.

6

Slocum approached the *Excalibur* with a feeling of dread, even though the sight of the brightly colored paddle boxes on either side of the vessel and the general bustle of men working had cheered him before. The meeting with Berton Fellows in the restaurant did not seem at all like a coincidence. But why would a shyster lawyer come seeking him out? Slocum didn't have a good explanation for that, except that the lawyer watched closely everything happening aboard the riverboat. He knew of Sam Jackson's death, he knew Slocum was the new owner, and he had to know Slocum wasn't cut out for the life of a river man. Not for an instant did Slocum believe the bull about the unnamed client wanting to pay exorbitant prices for either the *Excalibur* or its cargo. If Fellows tried anything violent to make him sell the *Excalibur*, Slocum knew the lawyer would hire someone and that it would be aboard the riverboat.

"There's something hidden *in* the cargo that makes it

valuable," he said, more to himself than to Eleanore. Since Fellows had offered eighteen thousand dollars, that made the hidden contraband worth more. Lots more. But what could it be? Slocum hardly believed anything but a pile of gold would be worth that much trouble, and he wasn't blind. There wasn't any spot aboard the *Excalibur* where that much gold bars or bullion could be stashed without being found during even the most cursory of examinations. A secret of that size would never be kept from the crew for very long, either.

"John, are you going to keep the *Excalibur?*" Eleanore asked, her voice almost shaking with pent-up emotion. The idea of knowing someone who owned a riverboat obviously thrilled the young woman. That he had been offered so much money for the boat thrilled her even more.

"What?" he said, his thoughts pulled back to the lovely dark-haired woman. "No, I meant what I told Fellows. I'll nursemaid the boat to St. Louis and turn 'er over to Marie Jackson."

"But you don't have to. I mean, it is yours. This Captain Jackson *gave* you the boat."

"No, I don't have to give it away, but I didn't do anything to earn it."

"That's a strange way of looking at it. Why not consider it God's will. Or just luck? If you found a twenty-dollar gold piece, would you go looking for its owner?"

"That's not the same thing, Eleanore. But if Sam had given me a double eagle, I'd as like take it to Marie Jackson as I would the *Excalibur*." To Slocum this seemed fair. Whatever sorrow and heartache Mrs. Jackson had put up with while Sam was on the river carried a price — and partial payment for it and a murdered husband had to be the riverboat.

"You're a strange one, John Slocum," the woman said. "Oh, no! There's Mrs. Hortense stalking along the deck. She must be looking for me. I'd better go."

"If you get into any trouble with her, just let me know,"

Slocum told her. "I'll straighten it out."

Eleanore looked pained. "John, Mrs. Hortense doesn't care for you one little bit. After you shot that rat in the ballroom, she's referred to you as 'that gun-happy upstart,' and once she even muttered something about you being a 'barbarian without any manners, whatsoever.'"

Slocum had to laugh. "She won't believe I'm the *Excalibur*'s owner, but if she gives you too much trouble, I'll make her walk the plank just like the old-time pirates did. Right over the side, into the muddy Mississippi. Splash!" Slocum demonstrated someone vainly swimming in the yellow murk.

"Be careful, John," Eleanore said as she hurried to find Mrs. Hortense.

Slocum hardly needed the young woman's advice. The waters he found himself in became increasingly turbulent. Sam Jackson dead. Himself shot at twice. The pilot murdered. The strange offer from Berton Fellows.

All he wanted to do was get to St. Louis, buy a horse, and ride due west. Even the desolation of the Great American Desert would look good to Slocum right now. He heaved a big sigh and started up the *Excalibur*'s gangplank. To get to St. Louis he had to travel up a long stretch of river.

"Howdy, Mistuh Slocum," came a cheerful voice. Slocum waved to Erasmus Washington. He noticed the other roustabouts sidled away from Washington when he did so.

Going on up the stairs to the passenger deck, carrying his store-bought clothes, Slocum spotted Leander Martin at the stern. The chief clerk spoke earnestly with someone hidden in shadows. Martin gestured wildly, obviously angry and upset, pointing up to the pilot house, then thrust his pointed finger down at the deck for emphasis. Only muffled sounds rose to Slocum.

Slocum stopped and watched, trying to catch sight of the man obscured by the shadows. Once an arm reached out, and he caught only a glimpse of cuff. It was as he expected.

The coat sleeve was elegant pearl-gray—the identical color of Berton Fellows's coat.

Slocum went up the stairs and into the ballroom. Captain O'Malley talked with a youngish man going prematurely bald. When Slocum entered, O'Malley motioned to him.

"Mr. Slocum, come along and meet the *Excalibur's* new chief pilot. This is Alexander duPont."

Slocum held out his hand. DuPont took it and gave a limp, sweat-damp handshake. Slocum didn't put much store in such things, but if a man didn't have a firm handshake he wasn't much of a man. Looking duPont over confirmed Slocum's worst suspicions.

Henry Sanders had been something of a peacock in dress. DuPont was no less flamboyant. His bright red silk shirt sported intricate designs woven into it, the green cravat was totally out of place, and the burgundy coat made Slocum want to squint as sunlight turned it into a beacon. The dark blue breeches were even tighter than the ones Sanders had favored, and the highly polished knee-high boots made Slocum think of darkly moving mirrors.

What put Slocum off most about the new pilot was his weasel face. It looked as if someone had grabbed hold and squeezed, the face flowing out into a snout equipped with sharp, pointed incisors and a tongue that nervously slipped in and out of his chapped lips. Accentuating the animalistic, scarcely human appearance was a waxed moustache whose tips curled upward in tight spirals.

"You made many trips up the river?" Slocum asked.

"Rather many, I might venture to say," said duPont.

"Mr. duPont came highly recommended," said O'Malley, "and, frankly, we didn't have much of a selection."

"There was no need to look farther when the best stands before you." DuPont executed a quick bow that made him look even more ridiculous.

Slocum drew O'Malley aside. He didn't want the new pilot to hear the question he was about to ask the captain.

"Who did the recommending?" Slocum knew the answer before Captain O'Malley spoke.

"Chief Clerk Martin. Seems the pair of them shipped together on the *J. M. White*."

"When was this?"

O'Malley looked at Slocum, eyes narrowing. Slocum was glad to see that the alcoholic fog had left those eyes. O'Malley looked sharper than he had at any time since walking onto the *Excalibur*.

"Odd question, Mr. Slocum."

Slocum turned back to duPont. "What boat did you and Martin serve together on?"

The pilot's eyes darted left and right, then fixed somewhere around Slocum's gunbelt. "We were on the *Natchez*. Best damn boat on the river, the *Natchez*."

"So I hear. Glad to have you piloting the *Excalibur*."

DuPont almost ran out of the ballroom. Slocum's eyes followed the man's gaudy track until duPont vanished through the carved wood doors and onto the outer walkway.

"What you gettin' at, son?" asked Captain O'Malley, scratching himself and working hard at looking unconcerned. "So what if him and Martin didn't remember the same on where they'd been together? Or maybe they were on both boats, both the *Natchez* and the *J. M. White*. Don't mean spit."

"Just a bit too convenient, the only pilot available being one recommended by Martin. I don't trust the man. And not just because he can't get his story straight."

"Is it duPont or Martin you don't trust?"

"Both." Slocum said nothing more as passengers began drifting out of their staterooms and into the ballroom. He pointed and asked, "How many?"

"Damn near a full house this trip," said O'Malley. "Forty cabin passengers and over a hundred deck huggers. Most of them deck passengers will be gone long 'fore we get to Baton Rouge, though. Might not be able to pick up more along the way, either. The *General Proctor* just passed by and might have scooped them all up ahead of us."

Slocum nodded, understanding that there were few wanting or needing to travel North. For a follower of the Stars and Bars, the jobs were in the South. Nothing waited for anyone from the wrong side of the Mason–Dixon line in the Northern factories or businesses.

"Have you checked the cargo?"

"I have. Your suspicions, sir, are unfounded. Everything is as it appears to be." Captain O'Malley turned and walked off without another word.

Slocum wasn't as sure as the captain about that. Fellows was no one's fool. He hadn't offered that handsome amount for the *Excalibur*—or just the cargo—from enlargement of the heart. Something of great value was hidden aboard the *Excalibur*. Slocum cursed Sam Jackson for not telling him what it was. Then he cursed the man for dying like he had.

Slocum went to his cabin and took in the luxury as if he had never seen it before. From the rude lean-tos he had slept under in the piney woods near Fort Smith, Arkansas, to the hollowed, hard ground with nothing more than a blanket under him that was his more customary resting place, this bed was like a piece of heaven's clouds ripped off and given to him. The thick carpets muffled his steps and the oil paintings on the walls spoke to him of distant lands he had never seen.

Slocum stripped off his battered clothing and held up the finery he had purchased, critically studying it in the full-length mirror.

Not as good as Fellows' duds, but not bad for a galoot like me, he decided. But Slocum didn't immediately don his new clothes. It had been a while since he'd had a good, hot bath. He slipped his old shirt and tattered trousers on and padded off barefoot to find the steward. A quick request produced a large tin tub and enough steamy hot water to scour off the worst of the grime.

Slocum settled into the hot water, tense at first, then

relaxing as the water soothed his tight muscles. He leaned
back, resting his head on the rim of the tub, and closed his
eyes. Although appearing to sleep, Slocum stayed alert. The
sound of his cabin door opening caused him to drop one
hand carelessly outside the tub. Dexterous fingers found the
worn ebony butt of his Colt Navy and held it behind the
tub, out of sight of his uninvited guest.

Slocum heard the door shut and the deadbolt slide home.
He opened one eye a slit and watched a dark form move
toward him. The Colt came up as Slocum pulled back the
hammer, cocking the gun.

"John!" came Eleanore's startled gasp. "I thought you
were asleep!"

"Didn't mean to startle you," he apologized, lowering
his pistol and releasing the hammer. "Get nervous when
I'm being stalked."

"Is that what I was doing?" the brunette asked mischie-
viously.

"I certainly hope so." He looked up at her, all too aware
of the way he responded to her presence. Slocum frothed
up a bit of the soapy water and let the suds hide the most
apparent reaction to Eleanore's trim, sleek beauty.

"Well," she said primly, sitting on the rim of the tub,
her hands folded in her lap. "I only came by to see if you
were all right. That nasty head wound might have left you
a tad dotty."

"Did I seem like I was out of my head?"

"I do declare, what else can it be when I hear a man turn
down eighteen *thousand* dollars?" she cried. "That's such
a princely sum."

"More'n I've ever seen in my life," admitted Slocum.

"Even if you wanted to turn the *Excalibur* over to Mrs.
Jackson, Mr. Fellows offered you eighteen hundred just as
agent. Are you opposed to honest money, John?"

"Can't say that a hard day's work ever seemed a waste
to me," Slocum told the woman, "but I doubt any money
coming from Fellows's wallet is honest."

"He did seem overly eager to get you to accept the money, and for no good reason. Who do you suppose his mysterious client is?"

Slocum had no ready answer for that. He had considered the possibility that there wasn't any anonymous buyer, that Fellows operated on his own to get the contraband Sam Jackson had agreed to smuggle North. One thing Slocum knew for sure: Leander Martin and Berton Fellows were in league.

That meant the new pilot was not to be trusted. But what could he do once the *Excalibur* steamed out into the river and started for St. Louis?

"Did you attend to Mrs. Hortense?" asked Slocum.

"Oh, yes, but she hardly missed me. It seems she and Captain O'Malley have struck up a fine friendship."

"The old dog," muttered Slocum.

"Mrs. Hortense is so distraught over Mr. Hortense," Eleanore went on, "that she is willing to look for comfort in any port."

"That's about where O'Malley has been, too—in every port." Still, Slocum couldn't fault the captain too much for the attentions he paid to Mrs. Hortense. As long as the portly woman was occupied with a genuine riverboat captain, gold braid gleaming on his sleeves, this left Eleanore Dahlquist free to be with the boat's owner.

Slocum liked the idea of having the whip hand more and more.

"The other passengers are so nice, also," Eleanore went on. She spoke of this and that, but her eyes watched attentively as the soapy froth floating on the tepid bath water began to dissipate.

"Haven't had the opportunity to talk with any of them." Some, such as the medicine peddler, James J. Poindexter, had been aboard the boat for several days awaiting departure. Most had arrived only this afternoon, to stay the night and leave in the early morning. The deck passengers would crowd on just before sailing, to stand packed shoulder to shoulder on the cargo deck amid the bales of cotton, tobacco, and other goods bound for St. Louis.

"There are so many interesting men among them," Eleanore said, fanning herself. The bubbles on the bath water began popping faster and faster now. "There's a hellfire-and-brimstone preacher by the name of Duggan haranguing any who will listen. I do believe the man has leather lungs. How he carries on! I do declare."

Eleanore tried not to look down into the bath as only a trio of large soap bubbles floated above Slocum's crotch. The man enjoyed the woman's coyness. It made him even harder, the tip of his erection poking up through the water now. The bubbles ringed it like pearls around a dowager's neck.

"There are a goodly number of gamblers, too," Eleanore went on. "Shifty-eyed men. I wouldn't advise you to sit in on any game where they were dealing the cards."

"All professional gamblers cheat," said Slocum. "They have to, if they want to keep eating. Even the best have the odds go against them."

"You sound very knowledgeable about cheating."

"I've done a share of it in my day," Slocum confessed, "but I prefer to play with men who don't have a grasp of odds. Saves putting blisters on my conscience."

"There you are again," Eleanore said in mock disgust. "A man with a sense of honor. You turn down *all* that money offered by Mr. Fellows and then you say you've gambled professionally but didn't cheat."

"Often," Slocum amended.

"You don't cheat often," Eleanore said in a low, seductive voice. "Is that all you don't do often?"

"There's one thing I don't do often enough," Slocum said, grinning broadly.

"And what might that be, John?"

He reached up and grabbed Eleanor's arm, pulling her into the bath. Water splashed everywhere and the brunette shrieked indignantly.

"Make love to you," he answered.

"My dress! You've got it all wet."

"Wouldn't want you to catch your death of cold, now would we? Better get out of those wet things right away."

"But my cabin is across the ballroom," she said, playing the game. "I can't cross that fine wood floor. Not dripping like this. It would ruin the floor."

"Then you're going to have to disrobe here and let your dress dry out before you leave."

"I do hope I can find something to keep me occupied while my clothes are drying," she said, her brown eyes twinkling.

"Something like this?" Slocum pulled her around. Their lips met and passionately crushed together. Eleanore made tiny sobs of joy and then broke off the kiss, awkwardly struggling up and out of the bath.

She dripped water on the carpet. Neither of them noticed. Eleanore began slowly stripping off her dress. Slocum stood to help her.

"Oh, John," she said. "How do you do it?"

"What?"

"Your fingers move with such sureness and yet they're sopping wet." Eleanore lifted one of Slocum's hands and kissed each finger tip, then began gently sucking on the fingers one at a time.

Slocum jerked even harder, his manhood beginning to hurt him. The woman did everything imaginable to excite him—and it all worked.

He guided his hand back to the front of her dress and continued working at the buttons until Eleanore shrugged her shoulders and stood naked to the waist.

"Pretty," he said. "So damn pretty there ought to be a law against it."

"It's all for you. Would you want to do anything against the law?" she teased.

"Wouldn't mind breaking into your bank and looting the vault," he said. His hand stroked over her skirt, pressing in at her crotch. The woman's hips began rotating slowly, grinding herself into the palm of his hand. Slocum felt the dampness of her arousal, an oiliness that differed from the water soaking the gingham dress.

"You sure are armed for it," Eleanore cooed, fingers tapping lightly at the man's organ. She stroked up and down the hardness and then ran her fingernails lightly over the hairy bag hanging below.

This was more than Slocum could stand. He scooped her up in his arms and twisted, tossing her through the air to land on the soft bed. Eleanore laughed as she rocked gently to and fro, her white arms held out in wanton invitation.

Slocum stepped from the tub and went to stand beside the bed. Tugging at her skirt got him nowhere. The catches on it eluded his fumbling eager fingers. He hiked up the cloth until it bunched around the woman's slender waist.

"Yes, John, yes, do it, yes!" she hissed. Eleanore sounded more like a snake than a woman. "Don't tease me. Do it!"

His strong hands parted the woman's thighs and lightly brushed over her undergarments. His own arousal was too great to take things easy now. Fingers looped under the frilly garment's waistband. Tendons stood out on his arms as he jerked, ripping them free to expose the delicate, pinkly pouting gates to a carnal paradise.

Eleanore rocked back on the bed, driving her shoulders into the mattress so that she could lift her behind. Slocum found this ideal for slipping into the woman's sexually heated interior. He sank all the way to his balls, then stopped, doing nothing but enjoying the sensation of being totally surrounded by her.

"Don't stop, John. It's driving me crazy. Move! Move!"

Slocum began a slow, deliberate motion, pulling back until only the tip of his hardness remained within her. They both gasped loudly for breath, bodies sweating, vision blurred. Eleanore shrieked in stark pleasure when Slocum moved forward once again.

Her hips went berserk. She squirmed about beneath the

man, pelvis driving upward to meet his thrust. Her fingers raked his back and pulled him over. Slocum went with the force of her passion, making certain not to slip free of his wondrous berth within her.

Eleanore's legs twined about his waist, holding them firmly locked together. Over and over they rolled, back and forth, bucking and hunching, until neither was able to stand even an instant more.

"Hard, John, drive into me hard. Give it all to me now."

"Just like breaking a starfishin' horse," he said. His lips closed on hers, moved to the wobbling breasts and tormented the pink caps on each, then fixed firmly on one earlobe.

The man felt the brunette tighten around him, squeezing down with a force that robbed him of all control. He burst apart and spilled his seed into her sucking depths. The bedsprings squeaked and protested under their combined weight until finally both were spent and unable to move.

Hanging onto her as if his life depended on it, Slocum began relaxing a mite.

"You're one hell of a woman, Eleanore," he told her, his eyes glowing. "It's a damn shame I didn't meet up with you sooner."

"Maybe not. The time's right for both of us, John. Before now I wouldn't have been ready."

"The memory of your husband?"

Eleanore nodded, a strand of dark hair falling into her eyes. Slocum brushed it away for her and pulled her even closer. Her soft breasts mashed against his bare chest, and her gentle breathing hotly teased his flesh.

The woman reached down and found faint stirrings again. She smiled and wriggled still closer, one slender leg going up and over Slocum's body.

A loud knock at the door caused them to jerk apart guiltily.

"Mr. Slocum, you in there?" came Sean O'Malley's voice. "Got to speak with you right away. We got trouble. The damn crew's deserted. We're not gonna be able to leave in the morning."

Slocum heaved a sigh. For all the good things about being owner of the *Excalibur*, there were a few bad ones, too. He patted Eleanore's bare bottom and swung to his feet, already working to climb into his trousers and face the new troubles brought him by the captain.

7

"Captain O'Malley, this had better be damned important," Slocum said angrily. He didn't enjoy having his recreation with Eleanore Dahlquist interrupted. "After all, I'm the owner of this riverboat—and you're the captain."

"It's important, son," said O'Malley, looking past Slocum to the unclothed Eleanore sprawled on the bed. The woman squirmed and pulled up the bedclothes to hide herself from the old man's gaze. When Slocum saw that O'Malley showed no interest in Eleanore's nakedness, he knew the matter was as serious as the captain made it out to be.

Slocum went out and closed the door behind him, pulling on his shirt as he went. He dropped his boots to the floor and then pulled them on. All the while he finished dressing, O'Malley had stood silently, nervously rubbing his hands up and down on his uniform coat.

"All right, Captain. Tell me about it."

"The roustabouts. They mostly quit just a few minutes

ago. Walked off without even a fare-thee-well. Said you was a jinx and that nobody aboard the *Excalibur* would reach St. Louis alive."

"They believed a rumor? Just like that?" Slocum knew there had to be more to it than O'Malley had revealed.

"Somebody claimed you was the one who murdered Jackson. That didn't set well with none of them, especially since it'd been in the backs of their feeble brains all along." O'Malley chewed on his lower lip and jerked his head, indicating he wanted to go outside. They left the ballroom and hung over the railing on the passenger walkway.

Slocum saw only a handful of roustabouts lounging about below on the cargo deck, and even these were not happy men. They looked glum, and one spoke in guarded tones to the others. Slocum watched and caught the gist of all that was being said, in spite of not being able to hear the words. Even the ones who faithfully stayed with the *Excalibur* had doubts.

"Jinx ship, they're sayin'," said O'Malley. "Murderer. And there's a lot more, but none of them will talk to me about it. Something about the Yankees wantin' to sink the *Excalibur*. Don't make a heap of sense, but then roustabouts don't think much about what they say before they say it."

"Can you replace them?"

"Replacing a roustabout is easy enough under ordinary circumstances. But, son these are not ordinary. No man wants to sign up on a ship where the new owner's supposed to have murdered the old one."

"The jinx, whatever it might be, is pretty damn effective, too," Slocum said angrily. "Saw it during the War. An entire company of cavalry refused to enter a valley just north of the Shenandoah because of ghosts. Somebody heard that there'd been an Indian burial ground in the valley, another heard Indian ghosts hated white men, another started putting it together, and soon enough no one would obey."

"What'd you do?"

Slocum shook his head tiredly. "Wasn't my company.

The lieutenant commanding couldn't do much more than skirt the valley. The Yanks got clean away by the time he'd travelled the extra fifteen miles."

"Getting a new pilot is gonna look easy compared to finding twenty roustabouts."

"Could we travel a ways up river, say to Baton Rouge, then do some hiring?"

O'Malley laughed and said, "You're too new on the river to appreciate this, but I'd wager there's not a man jack anywhere along the Mississippi who hasn't heard the rumors. They travel fast."

Slocum knew the captain exaggerated, but not by that much.

"Excuse me." Slocum went down the stairs to the cargo deck and motioned to Erasmus Washington. The black man ambled over after looking around the tight circle of grim, silent men around him.

"You want to talk to me, Mistuh Slocum?"

"I've heard the rumors. Can't say that I blame the crew who've left a hell of a lot. Just wanted to know why you and the others stayed. Must be a burden on you, shipping with a murderous owner aboard."

"Don't think you killed no one, Mistuh Slocum." Washington eyed him, then grinned. "Leastways, not Cap'n Jackson."

"Thanks for that, Ras. What about the jinx?"

"Don't never believe in them. My mama was a Jamaican nigger and she saw all the hoodoo and black magic there. Always said they was dealin' in fear, not real magic. Some things in this world I don't understand, some I don't want to, but jinxes? Ain't no such critters, Mistuh Slocum."

"What's Mr. Martin say about so many leaving?" Slocum asked.

Washington's eyes widened, but the man said nothing.

"You have any friends needing work at good wages? What were you getting under Sam Jackson? Fifty dollars a month?"

"Thass right, suh."

"Sixty dollars to new roustabouts, sixty-five to those of you who have stayed."

"Might take more'n money, Mistuh Slocum."

"You'd be in charge of them, Ras. Seventy-five dollars a month."

"Thass as much as the ship's carpenter earns," said Washington, thinking it over. "Mighty generous offer, Mistuh Slocum."

"How many men can you find before we sail in the morning?"

"For seventy-five dollars a month, I know I can find enough, Mistuh Slocum. Count on it."

"I'm counting on you, Ras. And thanks."

The man walked off, scratching at the stubble of beard and muttering to himself. Washington spoke to the roustabouts left. While their mood lightened a bit, it still had a ways to go before Slocum would count it as cheerful. But Washington worked with the crew, and soon they all walked down the gangplank and fanned out, heading into New Orleans.

Slocum wearily climbed the steps to the passenger deck. O'Malley still hung over the railing, gnawing at his lower lip.

"You put a fire in their boilers," the old captain observed. "Be nice if their head of steam got them moving in the right direction."

Slocum had nothing to add. He had faith in Erasmus Washington. The man struck him as a hard, honest worker. All they could do now was wait and see if he got results. If not, Slocum figured there was always Berton Fellows's offer to buy the *Excalibur*.

Without a crew or the hope of getting one, the *Excalibur* was as good as dead in the water.

"You surely do know how to pick 'em," said Captain O'Malley, admiration in his voice. "Washington got enough men together for us to sail. Won't be easy, but then, no trip upriver ever is. Just the nature of things."

"Leave in about six hours?" asked Slocum, glancing at his vest-pocket watch. The watch had once belonged to his brother Robert. When he had been killed, Slocum had sent the watch home to his parents. By the time he got back to Calhoun County, both his mother and father were long dead. The watch was a legacy of happier times for him.

"Seeing's how it's midnight now, you got the time figured to a tee," said O'Malley.

Slocum straightened the lapels of his new coat and looked around the ballroom. The band Sam Jackson had hired to play on the trip to St. Louis was straggling in, but their contract called for them to play only while the *Excalibur* was actually on the river. Most of the band members would use tonight as a last chance to tomcat around in New Orleans. The dining area stood off to one side, dominated by the white-jacketed stewards. The cook had yet to gear up fully for all the passengers; cold meats of various kinds had been put out for those who were waiting overnight. Of most interest was the bar set up at the other end of the ballroom. Sam had hired an independent to run it and the man set out a fine array of whiskey and what he called wine. His specialty was "French brandy," but Slocum hadn't had the heart—or the stomach—to try it yet.

What made Slocum smile, however, were the half-dozen men gathered around a gaming table. Already a game of faro taught ignorant men odds and made smart men richer. Slocum's quick eye picked out the two professional gamblers and how they were cheating and the eager passengers thinking they were lucky.

"What're the rules on gamblers?" Slocum asked the captain. "Do we let them cheat too much?"

"Can't stop them," said O'Malley. "Wouldn't want to, if we could. We collect ten percent of their winnings for letting them ride free to St. Louis."

Slocum nodded. The gamblers would lie about how much

they'd won, but even then the ten percent always totalled more than the price of their keep going upriver. The entire economy of a riverboat amazed Slocum. Everyone paid someone else for the right to work. If Erasmus Washington was an honest man—and Slocum figured him to be—he hadn't charged the new roustabouts more than ten dollars for the privilege of being hired onto a jinxed ship. Washington might even have lowered what was being offered as wages, intending to pocket the balance himself.

"Thinkin' on doing a bit of gambling yourself?" asked O'Malley. "Takes skill to come out on top of those sharps." He indicated the gamblers.

"They can fleece their own sheep. I'll keep my card games on a more moderate scale," said Slocum. He itched to get into a game. Something about the feel of the cards sliding off the freshly opened deck, the crisp sounds as they shuffled, the tension of betting, the small signs others gave off showing if they held good hands or bluffed—all that made Slocum come alive. Winning was everything. If money came along with it, that made it even better.

"I'm going to get some sleep," he told the captain. "But make sure a steward wakes me just before we leave. I want to be up in the pilot house watching."

O'Malley nodded and wandered off. Mrs. Hortense had made her grand entrance, and Captain O'Malley hurried to her side. Slocum saw nothing of Eleanore so he retired to his cabin. He entered, closed the door, and heard the soft sounds of naked flesh moving against linen sheets.

"We've got plenty of time, John," came the brunette's whisper. "Let's not waste it, though."

Smiling, Slocum took off his finery and climbed into bed next to the willing, wanton woman.

"Good day to leave New Orleans," said Captain O'Malley. The sky had turned leaden overnight and tiny drops of rain spattered against the decking and the glass windows of the pilot house. "The rain marks up the surface of the river so's you can tell the difference between wind marks and reefs."

"Silence in my house," grated Alexander duPont. The man blew into the speaking tube connecting the pilot house with the engineer. "Mr. Macallum, are you prepared?"

Slocum did not hear the answer, but it satisfied duPont. He tugged four times on a rope. Even over the gusty sighing of the steam engines, Slocum heard the bell ringing down below to signal for power. The paddlewheels began to move as heat built up in the boilers. DuPont jerked a wheel around and the double rudders behind the *Excalibur* bent to re-channel the flow of water driven backward by the paddle-wheels.

The *Excalibur* crept out into the sluggish flow of the Mississippi. Slocum had watched riverboats come and go for most of his life, but a thrill always came when he saw one leaving a dock. Being in the pilot house—*owning* the boat—made the thrill even greater for him.

DuPont tugged at the whistle. A mournful cry went up. A harder tug, and the whistle screeched in victory. The *Excalibur* moved into the main current, fought it, and won.

"We'll make Greenville, Mississippi, in about two weeks," said Captain O'Malley. "Till then, there's not much for me to do." He glanced at duPont, who was totally engrossed in guiding the *Excalibur* through the maze of smaller boats. Slocum wished the captain would keep a closer watch on the chief pilot, but he knew better than to mention it. If he'd learned nothing else about life on the river, he had found that the pilot held absolute power while the boat coursed up and down the river. The captain's job virtually ended until they docked again.

"There's no need to worry, Mr. Slocum," said O'Malley, grinning. "All our troubles are behind us—out there, in New Orleans. That's the fine thing about bein' on the river. You can sail away and leave your cares behind." O'Malley went off, whistling off-key.

Slocum studied duPont, hunched over the wheel, jerking on the jingler constantly to signal changes in power to the engineer, and worried even more. Slocum didn't think it was his imagination that duPont actually leered as he worked.

For five nights the band had played and the passengers danced. Slocum had avoided Eleanore during this time because of the way Mrs. Hortense hovered around her secretary. But his time hadn't been entirely idle. There were games on the tables—*his* tables, Slocum kept reminding himself—and excitement enough for any man.

He dealt the seven-card stud hand and watched the others drop out, one by one. All except one greenhorn fresh off a farm. Slocum was hardly an old man, but he was old enough and sophisticated enough to spot a man who was just itching to be separated from his money.

"You sure you want to keep playing?" he asked the farmer. The man nodded impatiently and pointed to the cards. Slocum shuffled and began the slow deal.

Slocum won consistently when he found out the farmer never folded. He played good hands and bad, and his bluffs were laughably poor. The sodbuster squinted and fidgeted, fingered his cards, and spat out the tobacco he chewed whenever he held a bad hand.

Slocum won bigger and bigger from him. The other players settled back to see how long it would take before Slocum cleaned the poor bastard of his last dime.

"A row of queens," Slocum announced, fanning them out. The farmer had nothing worth more than the spittoon full of tobacco juice.

"But you were bluffing," the farmer said. "I know you were bluffing."

"Not with three queens," Slocum said.

"Let it be, Harley. You're all tuckered out," said one of the other passengers.

"I can't afford to lose that money. I jist can't! What'd Bessie say if she finds out I upped and lost everything?"

"That you shouldn't gave got into a game in the first place," Harley's friend said in disgust. The man shook his head, rose, and stalked off, leaving Harley and Slocum alone at the table.

"You got to give me back the money, mister," said Harley. "It's all the money I had. I went to New Orleans 'cuz the bank there was the only one what'd loan me enough to keep the farm going. I can't go home and tell my wife I lost the money I borrowed."

Harley was shouting by this time. Slocum leaned across the table and said, "Calm down. You're old enough to know not to bet money you can't afford to lose. This was an honest game. I don't cheat. I don't have to."

"You . . . you're the owner of the boat, ain't you?"

"That's right."

"You got all the money you need. Gimme back what you took off me in the game. Give it to me!" Harley jumped to his feet, the chair crashing back onto the floor. The racket it made drew everyone's attention.

Slocum hadn't expected the farmer to pull a gun, but he did. Slocum stared down the barrel of an old Remington. Harley's hand shook so bad the pistol wobbled all over, sometimes centering on Slocum's head, more often not.

"Harley," Slocum said in a soft, soothing voice, "you don't want to start shooting. You're likely to hit a passenger. You don't have any call doing that. You don't have any call to stick that gun under my nose, either."

"I want my money back. Give it back! I need it!"

Slocum stayed calm. "Harley, let's step outside for a breath of air."

"The money!" The farmer grabbed for it, but Slocum pulled it away and stuffed it into his coat pockets. Wild-eyed, the farmer shoved the gun into Slocum's ribs.

"We talk outside. We don't want to disturb the other passengers."

Slocum got up and walked away. He relaxed a mite by the time he reached the door leading to the outer walkway; no bullet ripped apart his spine. Harley trailed behind, still intent on getting his money back. Slocum wasn't too pleased with any man fool enough to gamble without knowing what he was doing. He felt nothing but disgust for a man willing to rob to get back what he'd lost fair and square.

"The money. I need it." Harley jabbed the gun forward again.

"All right, farmer," said Slocum, measuring his words carefully. "I can't just give you the money back. That'd open me up to a world of trouble."

"What do you mean?" Harley sounded suspicious.

"Every man losing in a game would think he deserved the money back. Now," said Slocum, holding up a hand, "I recognize how it is with you. These are real special circumstances. It'd look as if the owner of a riverboat as big as the *Excalibur* had a soft heart if I just *gave* you my winnings. I got to keep discipline aboard the boat."

"So?" Harley sounded confused. Slocum kept waiting for the gun to point in some other direction so he could do something about it. Harley kept it level and dangerous.

"We go back in, like gentlemen, and play one more hand. Winner take all. I'll bet all you lost to me."

"But I ain't got anything to bet," wailed Harley.

"You got your gun. Your gun against my winnings." Slocum waited for the man's reaction.

"I guess that's the way to do it so's nobody gets in trouble," the farmer said.

They went back in, Slocum conscious of the pistol all the way to the poker table. He sat down. Harley sat across from him. Slocum pulled out a fresh deck, tore off the wrapper, and shuffled the slick cardboard. He let Harley cut.

"Here's the stakes," Slocum said, pushing the money to the center of the table. He waited until Harley dropped the gun onto the pile, then dealt.

A crowd gathered around the table. Slocum played, watched Harley, then took one card. When Harley called, Slocum dropped a full house onto the table, tens over eights.

"All I got is a pair of aces," Harley said.

Before the man looked up from his cards, Slocum reached out and pulled the pot toward him, money and gun. "Then you lose," Slocum said, his hand on Harley's gun.

"But . . ." The farmer sputtered and started to rise. Slocum signalled two stewards, who each grabbed an arm and pulled the kicking, shouting Harley from the room.

"That was smart thinking," said Captain O'Malley. "That boy was wound up tighter'n a two-dollar watch. If he'd kept that gun, he'd have shot half the people on the *Excalibur* and not even known what he was doing."

Slocum tossed the gun across to O'Malley. "Take care of this. Toss it into the river, give it back to him when we dock, I don't care."

"You're looking to put him off at the next stop?"

"I don't care if he has to walk on water to get home," said Slocum. He was mad that anyone showed so little common sense. "Harley's a danger to me and the passengers and a damn sight worse danger to himself. Maybe he'll learn."

"Doubt it," said O'Malley. "But his wife might beat the lesson into his worthless hide." The captain cocked his head to one side and asked in a low voice, "You wantin' him put off right now?"

"Dumped into the river?" This shocked Slocum. "No. Next time we dock is soon enough. He deserves to lose his money. He was foolish. But he also paid for his ticket. See that he gets a refund for the unused portion, if any."

O'Malley chuckled. "You'd've given him back the money he lost, wouldn't you, son?"

Slocum glared at O'Malley, angry that the man saw him so clearly.

"You would have," O'Malley went on, "but you don't like being pushed. If he'd begged and pleaded but acted enough like a man about it, you'd have given it all back."

"No one sticks a gun in my ribs," said Slocum. More quietly, he added, "You're right. If he'd convinced me his family was going to starve without the money, I would have returned it. Maybe I'd call it a loan. But when he started waving that gun around, threatening people who had nothing to do with his foolishness, I knew better than to give him more than a kick in the britches."

"For such a hard man, you can be pretty soft," said O'Malley.

Before Slocum could answer, the *Excalibur* lurched hard and threw them to the floor. Slocum skidded a few feet on the highly polished wooden dance floor. The band members went down in a pile of shouts and squeaking instruments and the passengers became hysterical.

"No need for alarm, folks," called out Captain O'Malley. The man's powerful voice shook off the grip of fear. The passengers quieted.

"What happened?" demanded one.

"Leastways they're asking and not shouting," O'Malley muttered so only Slocum could hear. Louder he asked, "Nothing to worry about. I'll go up to the pilot house and ask why the damn fool pilot's not giving us a smoother ride. Go on back to your dancin'. You were doing just fine, and the boat's stopped jerking around now." O'Malley signalled for the band to strike up a lively tune.

O'Malley and Slocum went outside and started up the stairs to the pilot house.

"What happened?" Slocum asked. "The *Excalibur*'s not moving."

"Unless I miss my guess," said O'Malley, "Mr. duPont has run us aground."

Slocum turned cold inside. Nothing was more helpless than a riverboat stranded on a sandbar. The treacherous currents of the Mississippi would rip them apart and leave behind only splinters unless something was done fast.

8

"You aimin' to get us all killed?" demanded Sean O'Malley. "This is the goddamnedest, stupidest, most..." O'Malley trailed off, sputtering incoherently. Slocum could see that the man wanted to grab duPont around the neck and choke him to death. Only through great restraint did O'Malley hold back.

Slocum showed no such restraint. He reached out, grabbed duPont by the shoulder, and shoved the man back against the wall of the pilot house—hard. Slocum heard the pilot's teeth rattle together and took some pleasure in that.

"What happened?" he said in a voice so menacing that Alexander duPont blanched.

"The fog. The sandbars shift. How was I to know? This is not my fault. The river, she is at fault. Ask anyone who has real experience." DuPont sneered again. His weasel eyes darted from Slocum to O'Malley and back. Nothing but contempt radiated from the man.

Slocum released him. "What about it, Captain? Could it happen the way he said?"

"Pilots are supposed to know the river. We're not far enough up to be in dangerous territory."

"The river shifts everywhere," the dandy cried. "The fog obscures my sight!"

"You have to be nearly blind not to see that," raged O'Malley, pointing.

Slocum frowned. He wasn't sure what O'Malley meant. Then he saw ripples pulling away from the far end of the sandbar. He remembered what O'Malley had said about leaving dock in the rain. The drops hitting the surface made it obvious whether the ripples were from wind or a sandbar.

These were from a sandbar. And the *Excalibur* had run squarely onto it.

"What do you have to do to get us off?" Slocum asked the captain.

"Reverse engines. We'll try that first." O'Malley pulled the cork plug from the speaking tube, blew into it to get the chief engineer's attention, then shouted, "Mr. Macallum, how long to reverse?"

O'Malley put the tube to his ear, listened, then recorked the speaking tube and glared at duPont. To Slocum he said, "He can get the cam rods reversed in about an hour. The job's got to be done by apprentices." O'Malley glared at the pilot again.

Slocum and O'Malley went out onto the hurricane deck and looked forward at the sandbar holding the *Excalibur* up and out of the flowing river.

"Reversing the cams is a damn dirty job. And time consuming when we've schedules to meet," grumbled O'Malley. "Not necessary. None of it. The son of a bitch should have avoided the 'bar."

"When Macallum gets the engines reversed, can he pull us off without any trouble?"

O'Malley snorted. "Paddlewheels can't pull us off. We reverse and the paddles send water up and under the *Ex-*

calibur and get us afloat again. The crew has to pole us off, if they can."

"What happens if that doesn't work?"

"You *are* a newcomer. We try to warp off. One of the crew plants a 'dead man' and then we use the forward steam capstan to pull us off." O'Malley answered Slocum's unspoken question. "The 'dead man' is nothing more than a railroad tie. Longer, but still a tie planted into the sandbar. It all comes down to a heap of trouble when it wasn't necessary."

"The fog is heavy," said Slocum. "I'm not making excuses for duPont, but it might be an accident."

"Fog's light."

Slocum wondered at that. Visibility was less than a hundred yards. The pilot had little enough time to identify a danger in the water, much less get the *Excalibur* shifted left or right with the balky rudders before running aground. But Slocum had to rely on O'Malley's expertise.

Sean O'Malley had dried out. Slocum hadn't seen the man take a single drink since the *Excalibur* left New Orleans, though the captain must have been sorely tempted. He had attended to all the myriad details of running the riverboat with a flair that showed how much he enjoyed being on the Mississippi once more. Slocum decided duPont had committed a sin no competent pilot would.

Slocum left the captain and went down to the cargo deck. As he stepped off the stairs, he overheard Erasmus Washington talking with several of the other roustabouts.

"Saw the 'bar, plain as day, I tell y'all," insisted Washington. "How a pilot could heave us up onto that 'bar is somethin' beyond me."

"He didn't have the curtains down on the forward ports. Saw lights glarin' out, just like day," said another.

"Crazy bastard is tryin' to kill all of us. They was right about what they say back in New Orleans. This is a jinx boat."

"Stop sayin' that," Washington ordered.

"Ah kin stop sayin' it, but that don't stop it from being true, Ras. Ah got greedy what with all the money you offered. Don't do no good bein' rich if'n you're dead. Dead men don't spend their earnings."

"Mr. Washington, said Slocum, letting his boot heels click loudly against the deck as he swung on down from the stairs. "A word with you."

"Yes, suh."

Away from the other crewmen, Slocum asked the man, "How long you been on the river, Ras?"

"Well nigh all my life, one way or another, Mistuh Slocum. Worked on the docks, took on some work aboard the barges. After the War I started up on these heah steam riverboats."

"Did duPont ground us on purpose?"

"Now, suh, I can't answer a question like that. Not meanin' to be disrespectful, suh, but I ain't no pilot." Washington backed away.

"I think I got answer enough. Thank you."

"What you goin' do, Mistuh Slocum?"

"Nothing right now, Ras, except stand back and watch how you get the *Excalibur* off the sandbar."

The man laughed and pointed at the array of pulleys and ropes being strung along the sides of the stranded, helpless riverboat. "Those'll get us off the 'bar, Mistuh Slocum. Just you wait and see."

Slocum blinked, then settled down to see how the feat would be accomplished. Washington and the others finished with the rigging and waited for Captain O'Malley's orders.

Before O'Malley shouted down his commands, Leander Martin stalked out. Slocum faded back into the shadows and observed. Martin grabbed a roustabout who had stayed with the *Excalibur* and spun the burly man around. Slocum waited for the roustabout to drop Martin with a single punch. Martin was slender and even puny appearing next to the deckhand.

No fight started. The roustabout shook his head and

pointed up to the pilot house, then out into the dark. Martin's agitation caused him to raise his voice. All Slocum caught was, "... where the hell are they? He did his job just fine. You were supposed to see to..."

The rest of Martin's words were drowned in the rush of the *Excalibur*'s engines reversing. Slocum felt the riverboat rising up as water rushed from the stern forward, propelled by the twin paddlewheels on either side of the boat. Huge clouds of foam rose around the riverboat, water beaten to froth between wood hull and soft sand.

"All hands," called down Captain O'Malley, "prepare to spar off the sandbar!"

Washington and the others pulled long iron-tipped timbers off the deck and placed the shod end onto the sand. Using the pulley arrangement, the men tugged and strained until the ropes were taut. The line was then draped around the steam capstan and Washington started it up. Turn by slow turn, the twisting motion pulled in the rope and slid the *Excalibur* along the treacherous sandbar.

"More steam!" shouted O'Malley. "Mr. Macallum, get 'the doctor' working harder. *More steam!*"

Slocum went around and peered over the edge down to the boiler deck. He saw a small steam-fed pump being hand-tended; it was used to fill the boilers with water. Slocum guessed this was the "doctor" O'Malley mentioned. All the engineers worked with a vengeance to keep their hot charges at full capacity. The paddlewheels churned and drove water forward, and the steam capstans continued to pull on the tackle that Washington had set.

The *Excalibur* lurched heavily, and Slocum fell against a bale of cotton. From above came the loud cry, "We've warped off the 'bar. Keep pulling, damn your eyes, keep pulling until the paddles are free!"

Slocum waited until the order was given for the engines to shut down. He felt the drifting sensation as the *Excalibur* was caught by the river current and lightly wafted along. The ponderous bulk of the boat seemed little more than a leaf to the power of the Mississippi.

"Mr. Macallum," commanded Captain O'Malley, "reset the engines. Please notify me when the cams are reversed and ready for normal running."

The engineer acknowledged. The others in his crew grumbled, but began the back-breaking work of pulling the cams free and resetting them.

Slocum took the steps up to the pilot house in twos, out of breath by the time he arrived. O'Malley loudly berated duPont, then spun and left the pilot alone in the house.

"He won't do it again, he says," mimicked O'Malley. "The ignorant son of a bitch!"

"You trust him enough to let him continue?" asked Slocum. He didn't trust duPont farther than he could throw him. Off the hurricane deck that amounted to less than thirty feet.

"A pilot's got his prerogatives," O'Malley said glumly. "I ought to get Smithson and let the boy continue. He's got good sense, that Smithson. But I can't overtax him. Got to let duPont show us if this was just an accident or damn foolishness on his part."

"He might take us all to the bottom," said Slocum. "That's a mighty big risk."

O'Malley shrugged. He obviously did not like the idea of leaving duPont in the pilot house, either, but the way things were done on the river looked well nigh unchangeable.

Slocum returned to the ballroom, then went to his cabin and fell into a troubled sleep. He had nightmares of being crushed under tons of wet river sand and having bales of cotton stuffed into his mouth. He awoke just before dawn, drenched in a cold sweat.

Slocum leaned over the railing and watched as the *Excalibur* slipped into the tiny dock. Captain O'Malley and duPont had got into a knock-down-drag-out fight over making this stop. In the end, the captain had prevailed. The riverboat cut the engines and the drag of water against the stationary paddles acted as a brake. DuPont did pull them in smartly, Slocum had to grant.

"We'll let off some of the squeamish passengers," O'Malley said, coming up beside Slocum. "There's even one poor fool on the dock wanting passage upriver, just a few dozen miles."

"Are you putting that farmer off?"

O'Malley pointed. Erasmus Washington and two of the burly roustabouts were dragging Harley from the cargo deck onto the rotting dock. He shouted and fought, but in their strong grips he was as ineffective as a willful child trying to disobey his parents. Washington gave a huge shove and sent the man sprawling.

"You can't do this!" shouted Harley.

"You got your passage money given back," said Washington, enjoying himself. "Don't make us take it for our trouble. Goodbye, suh."

Harley brushed dirt off his overalls and stood cursing under his breath. He started off, never once even looking back at the *Excalibur*.

"He hasn't learned a damn thing," sighed Slocum.

"You're not in the business of educating idiots," pointed out Captain O'Malley. "He ought to be thankful he's still got wind enough to breathe. Most owners would've draped a line around his ankle and dragged him upriver."

"I'll learn," promised Slocum. "Next time it happens . . ."

"Bullshit," O'Malley said cheerfully. "You got too good a heart for that. In spite of being hard on the outside." O'Malley paused, sucked at his gums, then said, "Maybe that's why you take pity on fools like the farmer. You've seen too much violence, too much robbing and killing."

"How long before we push on?"

"Depends on how bad these landbound crooks hold us up. Chief Clerk Martin says they're askin' damn near three dollars a cord for their wood. Two and a half is robbery, but three?" O'Malley spat.

"How much do we need?"

"Not much. We haven't been running that long. The engineer keeps the boilers and engines in good repair, so we don't lose much steam. We been using about twenty-five cords a day. A couple ranks would do us just fine."

Slocum peered out over the railing and down to the boiler deck with the long rows of wood. He watched as the roustabouts brought aboard the wood, twenty cords per rank, each rank over eighty feet long—almost a quarter the length of the entire riverboat.

"We'd better afford the wood if you hadn't got so damn generous with offering Washington that handsome pay. I had budget fixed at eleven thousand, five hundred for the trip. We're going to run over. Way over."

"Don't worry that much about a profit," said Slocum. He patted his coat pocket. "I've made close to five hundred dollars off the tables."

"That don't help me balance my books," complained O'Malley. Slocum smiled. O'Malley talked as if the *Excalibur* were his. Anew, Slocum felt good about choosing the down-and-out Confederate Navy captain to run the *Excalibur*. O'Malley had dried out and fallen back into military ways, and ran a taut ship.

Except in the matter of Alexander duPont.

"Is Smithson going to take us out?" asked Slocum.

"Still Mr. duPont's province."

After almost an hour, a full forty cords of wood had been added to the eight-foot-high stacks on the boiler deck. As he watched, O'Malley mumbled about going over to coal, like some of the others had done. Slocum had no opinion one way or the other. He left O'Malley and went to watch the chief engineer supervising an apprentice using a drag chain to clean the scale off a flue.

"You, there," bawled Macallum; "get the mud drum clean before we leave dock. Do it, damn your eyes!"

Slocum saw a skinny youth shudder, then begin the nasty chore. Slocum stood nearby.

"Need any help?" he asked.

"Naw, this ain't hard. Just messier'n shit." The youth pulled open the filters and scooped out handfuls of smelly, oozing yellow mud sucked out of the river water. He dumped it overboard and went back for another load.

"How often do you clean them?" Slocum marvelled at the amount of muck collected.

"Five, six times a day."

When the youth finished, he dropped in exhaustion and dangled his feet over the edge of the boat. He called over to Slocum, "You want a drink?"

"Sure." Slocum had been in the hot sun for some time, trying to get a better understanding of what went on aboard the boat.

He wasn't prepared for what happened. The youth dipped a bucket over the side and pulled up muddy water from the river.

"Damn stuff is too thick to navigate and too thin to cultivate. All that's left is to drink it." The boy sucked up a huge quantity of the water, made a face, and passed it over to Slocum. Slocum hesitantly sampled it; the water tasted as bad as he'd thought it would.

"Thanks."

The youth shrugged and heaved himself to his feet. "Got to get back to work. Macallum's a damn slave driver. Next you know he'll have us rowin' up the river like one of them damn Roman slave ships."

The *Excalibur* shuddered as steam built up in the boilers once more. The three-hundred-fifty-foot-long-boat turned slightly, then shivered all over like a dog shaking off water and headed back into the center of the river.

"About time," O'Malley said as Slocum rejoined him. "DuPont has been dragging his ass all over, trying not to leave. I may just throw him overboard yet and make do with Smithson. Might even take a turn or two myself. Been years since that was necessary."

"During the War?"

"Lost my pilot to a Yankee gunboat. Filled us full of holes so's we were almost at the point of sinking. But I navigated us through and we delivered the supplies. *Then* we sank." O'Malley laughed. "Don't look so glum. We won't sink. Bright, sunny day like this? Never happen."

Slocum had a feeling in his gut that refused to go away. No matter how reassuring Sean O'Malley was, he felt a sense of foreboding. Slocum retired to his cabin for a while, cleaned his Colt Navy, loaded it, and found its mate and serviced it, too. With one pistol in his cross-draw holster and the other stuck into his belt, Slocum rested easier.

But not much. And just at sunset his fears proved justified.

Shots rang out, sounding loud even above the constant churning of the paddlewheels. When the engines stopped, the gunfire became the dominant sound. Slocum rushed into the ballroom, looked up and down, and saw curious passengers. No one understood that something was wrong. Not yet.

"John," called out Eleanore Dahlquist, coming from her cabin next to Mrs. Hortense's, "what's wrong? I thought I heard gunshots."

"Stay in your cabin and don't come out till I tell you. Might be nothing."

"It's not," she said. "You wouldn't act this way if you didn't think we were in trouble."

"Get into your cabin and lock the door," he ordered. Eleanore surprised him by giving him a quick kiss. The brunette turned and dashed not to her cabin but to Mrs. Hortense's. Slocum shook his head. All Eleanore might do would be to keep the portly woman from getting too hysterical. He doubted even God Almighty could do that.

He went quickly out onto the walkway and peered into the gloomy twilight. He heard the slurshing noises of moving keelboats before he caught sight of their dim silhouettes moving alongside the *Excalibur*. Slocum drew his Colt and waited to use it.

He blinked, almost blinded, when a long tongue of flame leaped forth from the shadows. A man aboard the *Excalibur* gasped; a splash sounded. Slocum knew one of his crew had been wounded and had fallen overboard. With the Mississippi's current running as swiftly and creating such a powerful undertow as it did, the man had probably drowned before he bobbed to the surface.

Another yard-long lance of bright orange flame showed. Slocum raised his Colt, cocked the hammer, and sighted, figuring where the shadowy gunman would be. His .31-caliber slug blasted forth and produced a stream of curses. He had no way of telling whether he'd done any real damage, but the pirates now knew they'd be in for a fight. That might slow them down long enough for O'Malley to get the crew organized to repel any trying to board the *Excalibur*.

"That you, Slocum?" came O'Malley's voice. "Thought so. You're the only one carrying a gun."

"Got two. Need my spare?"

"Keep it. Got my own." O'Malley hefted one of Sam Jackson's double-barreled shotguns. From the bulges in the captain's uniform pocket, it appeared that he had stuffed all the available shells in and was prepared for a long fight.

"How often does this happen?" Slocum demanded.

"Too often, but usually not like this. We're in the middle of the river. Usually any riverboat can outsail those keelboats."

"Why were the engines cut off?"

O'Malley didn't answer.

"Did duPont order it?"

"Yes," said Sean O'Malley, his voice grim and edged in steel. "Said there was a problem with the safety valve. Mr. Macallum denies it."

"Pirates wait for a boat to run into a sandbar, don't they?" asked Slocum.

"That's the way they operate. Get the victim helpless, then pluck it like a ripe fruit."

The part of the argument Slocum had overheard where Martin had claimed to be ready but something had gone wrong looked more damning by the instant. If duPont had intended for them to be boarded while on the sandbar, but Martin had failed to organize the pirates in time—or if duPont had run aground on the wrong sandbar—much made sense.

Slocum would attend to it. Later. After the pirates had been driven off.

"Can't see what they want," grumbled O'Malley. "No cargo worth stealing, and the passengers don't look to be as rich a lot as those normally travelling the river."

The shotgun roar drowned out any reply Slocum might have given. The orange tongue lashed into the gathering darkness and the heavy 00 buckshot found a target. A man let out a soul-tearing shriek and tumbled off the cargo deck and into the river. A second barrel missed its target. O'Malley levered open the breech, ejected the spent cardboard casings, and stuck in two more shells.

"This is going to be a long night," he said.

"Get us moving. I'll see to removing our non-paying guests," said Slocum. He dropped down the steps three at a time and landed on the cargo deck in a crouch. Bullets whined just above his head. His Colt spat leaden death. His unseen bushwhacker crumpled forward out of the darkness, dead.

Slocum went to him and rolled him over. The man wore clothes common to river men and carried a gun that might have been a duplicate of the one Slocum held in his hand. Slocum picked it up and stuck it into his holster. There would be no time to reload the percussion caps, bullets, and charge; the extra gun could be put to good use.

"Mistuh Slocum?" came Erasmus Washington's voice. "That you?"

"Here, Ras. What's the situation look like?"

"Maybe ten, fifteen of them cocky bastards climbed up onto the boiler deck. Think they might have released the head of steam to make us dead in the water."

Slocum cursed. All O'Malley's work would be for nothing until they recharged the boilers.

"'Bout eight of the crew dead or sore wounded," Washington said. He swung a baling hook back and forth. The worn tip gleamed a wicked silver in the dim light filtering out of the boat's ballroom above.

"Let's go change the odds in our favor," said Slocum.

"Thass the way I like to hear a man talkin'," said Washington. "Thass the way Cap'n Sam always said it."

Slocum fired once, twice, a third time before he hit a man lifting a length of wood as a club. Washington stepped behind Slocum, grunted, and twisted away. Slocum glanced back and saw that the roustabout had buried the wicked hook in a pirate's groin. The man jerked about trying to pull the curved hook free from his body. He died before he succeeded.

"Some folks just don't know when to die," said Washington.

"Thanks. I think he wanted to bury that in my back." Slocum pointed to a knife on the deck. Washington scooped it up, but Slocum noticed he didn't toss away the baling hook. Washington stayed with the weapon he was most familiar with.

"Around the boilers. There!" Washington pointed. Slocum had already spotted the problem. Four men crouched near the brick-lined boiler. They had released the steam through the safety valve, then defeated the safety-valve arm by weighting it down with spare firebricks.

"No way we're leaving without them out of the way," said Slocum. "Stay here and I'll see what can be done."

"No way, Mistuh Slocum. I enjoys a good fight as much as the next man."

"Walk quiet, then, and protect our backs." Slocum's full attention turned to moving through the forests of firewood and doing it silently. He hesitated, checked his Colt, then stepped out. He gave the men no chance to fight. A single shot killed the one on the left. Then the hammer fell on a spent chamber. The captured pirate's gun in his left hand flew straight across while the empty Colt went up and over in a border shift. Two more bullets scattered the remaining three men. Slocum flat-out missed, the pirate's gun not being trued in and firing up and to the left.

Slocum's spare Colt came out. Four shots were needed to kill another pirate. Then Slocum was bowled over as the last two charged. They thought to make short work of him. Slocum caught sight of Erasmus Washington towering above like a black juggernaut. A mighty hand swung the baling hook, lifted one of the pirates off the deck, and held him suspended, feet kicking feebly.

Slocum caught the other man by surprise as he gawked at Washington. A quick punch to the throat sent the man to his knees, gagging. Slocum rose, kicked, and connected the toe of his boot with the pirate's chin. A sick crunching told the story; he had broken the man's neck.

"Best to get rid of this trash," said Washington. He heaved and the man on the baling hook flew through the air, over the rail of the boiler deck, and into the night-shrouded waters of the Mississippi. For a moment, Washington and Slocum stood, saying nothing, panting heavily. The sounds of O'Malley's shotgun came like springtime thunder, then died away.

"How do we fix the boiler?" Slocum asked.

Washington kicked the bricks off a rope holding a long metal arm. The hissing told of steam pressure mounting inside once again. The safety valve had been closed.

"Be a few minutes 'fore this one has enough head," said Washington. "Lemme find Mr. Macallum. He can get us movin' 'fore you know it."

Slocum curtly nodded. He had other tasks to do. Cautiously mounting the steps, he checked out the cargo deck. All quiet. Farther up to the passenger deck. No signs of fighting. To the texas deck. Nothing. To the hurricane deck and the pilot house. It sounded as if Shiloh was being re-fought.

"Damn it, duPont there was no call to shut us down. Not in the middle of the damned river!" raged Sean O'Malley.

"In my opinion as pilot, there was," the man said.

Slocum didn't want to get involved. This fight didn't immediately threaten the *Excalibur*. He went back down to the passenger deck to find Eleanore and make sure she was unharmed. Just before he entered the ballroom, he heard Leander Martin's voice.

". . . they botched it. They knew better! We had the chance before."

The crewman he talked to Slocum recognized as a roust-about. "Mr. Martin, that ain't none of my doing. You and the pilot had better get it all squared away between y'all. I done what I was told."

Slocum moved to confront them but the *Excalibur* gave a lurch, causing him to scrape a pistol along the railing. This small sound alerted both the crewman and Martin. They were gone by the time he reached the door leading into the ballroom.

The *Excalibur* shivered again and the forty-foot-diameter paddlewheels began turning once more. They moved against the current and soon outpaced any keelboat. Slocum entered the brightly lit room and went to find Eleanore.

The time was at hand for him to confront both Martin and duPont. But first he'd see to Eleanore.

9

"O Mark Four!" came the cry. Slocum craned his neck around and tried to see the man crouching at the port side of the *Excalibur* with the weighted, knotted rope in hand to measure the depths.

"Four fathoms," said Captain O'Malley. "We're doing well. And it's damn well about time. Those pirates!" He cleared his throat, spat, and shook his head. "Damnedest thing I ever saw, in all my years along the river."

Slocum stayed quiet. He turned over and over all the possibilities, and the only one that amounted to a hill of beans came down to Leander Martin being responsible for the pirate raid. He had sought out the chief clerk, but O'Malley had demanded his immediate attention.

What to do with Alexander duPont proved a weightier problem. The pilot had run them aground and, in the middle of the river, had cut the engines and ordered the steam in the boilers released. They had been sitting ducks for the pirates. To let the man continue as pilot was suicidal.

O'Malley and Slocum had decided that young Smithson's shifts would be expanded, and that duPont would continue standing watches, but under O'Malley's scrutiny. It was little enough, but it had to suffice until they reached a port where the pilot could be replaced.

"O Quarter Less Three!" came the cry.

"The river's getting shallower," said O'Malley. "We're down to sixteen and a half feet now. But there's still plenty of clearance, son," the captain told Slocum when he saw the worried look on his face. "Even loaded, the *Excalibur* only has a six-and-a-half-foot draft."

"O Quarter Less Twain!"

Slocum gripped the railing as the *Excalibur* dragged bottom. Five feet—and O'Malley had said they needed six and a half.

"Don't worry, son, not yet. Not yet. Smithson will keep us going forward at full speed so's our momentum will carry us over the rough spots. We might be able to slip right on over the sandbar. This is old hat even for a kid like him. Fact is, he might be doin' this better than an old timer. There's stories galore along the river about ingrained habits doin' old pilots in."

Slocum started to speak, but the captain kept up a steady flow of words.

"Used to be a right nasty spot along the river where the fog hung so thick you could cut it with a knife, drop it in a bowl, and suck it up as pea soup. Yes, sir, it was that thick—and there was no pilot with eyes what could see through it. But we didn't need to.

"That stretch of the river was blessed by the barkingest dog what ever lived. He'd hear a riverboat steamin' up and he'd commence to barkin' something fierce. A good pilot depends on his ears as much as on his eyes—more, in fog. The pilot knew where the bend in the river was by the way the dog barked and learned to navigate blind, fog or no fog."

Slocum licked dry lips. He tried not to listen to the calls from the deckhand shouting out the depth readings.

"Well," continued O'Malley, "the pilot finds himself in the worst fog that ever hid the river. He knows he's gettin' close to the bend, but he has no idea how close. Thinks it's a ways up. He blows the whistle four, five times, and waits for the dog to bark.

"Well, sir, the dog never barked. Not once. The pilot ordered full steam ahead, thinking he had a ways to go. Blows the whistle again a few minutes later. No bark. And, by gum, he smashes his boat square into the bend, beaches her so hard it took four dozen men almost two days to dig under her and get water flowing so's to lift the boat up enough. Worst grounding in years."

"Why'd he miss the dog's signal?" asked Slocum.

"That's the strange part," said O'Malley. "The dog always barked without fail—except that night. But there was a reason. And a good one it was, too. The dog had upped and died three days prior."

"This is supposed to reassure me?" asked Slocum.

"No, just give you a feel for what might happen along the river if you're not sharp all the time."

"Thanks," Slocum said sarcastically. "Now you can tell me what'll happen if we can't clear this sandbar we seem to have got lodged on?"

"Then we spar off and we've lost another damned two hours."

Slocum was worried. The pirates who hadn't been killed were only driven off. The keelboats had been filled with them as they slipped back into the shadows of night along the Mississippi. While he doubted they had kept up with the riverboat, the possibility existed that other pirates were in league with Martin and duPont.

The *Excalibur* groaned and spars creaked in protest as the flat bottom raked along the sandbar. O'Malley didn't look upset when the creaking became outright crunching.

"O Quarter Less Twain!" came a new cry.

"Still maintaining bottom," said O'Malley. "We're going to make it. The sandbar isn't large enough to stop us."

"O Mark Two!"

Slocum looked at O'Malley, who smiled.

"O Mark Four!"

"We made it," said O'Malley, heaving a deep sigh, the first sign that he had entertained any doubts about the riverboat's safety.

"Nooooooo Bottom!"

"We are clear," the captain said. "This has been one hell of a night, Mr. Slocum. I suggest you go get some sleep. We may all need rest before this trip is at an end."

Slocum shook his head. "Got to find Martin. He and duPont are in this together. I won't go so far as to say they plotted to have Sam Jackson killed, but they know something about it. And Martin is going to tell me all about it."

"Son, that expression you got plastered on your face frightens me. Downright ugly, it is. I don't reckon I'd like to be in Mr. Martin's boots right about now."

"You deal with duPont. Martin is all mine."

"I may be captain of the *Excalibur,* but you're the owner," O'Malley said with some satisfaction. "You won't hear argument from me on this account."

Slocum touched the ebony grip of his pistol. He had spent close to fifteen minutes quickly cleaning it and reloading. It wouldn't fail him if called on for service. Slocum hoped it wouldn't come to that. If he started firing, men started dying. With Martin dead, there'd be one less source of information about Sam Jackson's death, the bushwhackings Slocum had barely lived through, the pirate attack, and the mysterious cargo that must be at the heart of the matter.

Slocum went down from the pilot house where Mr. Smithson stood smiling, the riverboat under his sure control, to the cargo deck. Something told Slocum this was where he'd find the chief clerk. A man stirred at the prow of the boat. Slocum froze, listening, hand on his Colt.

"Oh, rollin' up de river,
Steamin' at de moon,
Chase de possum up de bank
And cook de grizzlum coon."

The words came, melodic and soothing. He recognized Erasmus Washington's voice. He turned from Washington and toward the stern of the *Excalibur* and the bales of cotton rising like some full-sized maze. Slocum had seen pictures of English mansions where the gardens had hedges cut into mazes. The way Martin had stacked the cotton bales reminded him of this.

Slocum entered one narrow corridor and cocked his head to one side, listening hard. Over the pounding of the paddlewheels against the muddy water came a different noise: leather against wood decking. Softly, he slipped forward, eyes darting left and right and occasionally up to the tops of the bales. Slocum had hunted and been hunted by enough Indians to know the danger of not playing attention to *all* directions. A man falling from a tree limb—or from the top of a cotton bale—could knock him senseless before he knew what hit him.

He knew. He'd done it enough times himself.

A dark form crossed in front of him, going from left to right along a crossing corridor in the cotton bales. Slocum drifted to the intersection, making less noise than a whisper. While he failed to make out the man's identity, he heard a clanking of glass on glass and smelled a pungent odor that wrinkled his nose.

It took Slocum a few seconds to remember where he'd smelled that vile stench before.

"The Latest Discovery of Science," he muttered. "The Old Indian Root and Herb Remedy, as supplied by the peddler." Slocum concentrated, struggling with the face, then remembered the name. "James J. Poindexter."

Slocum frowned. What was the patent-medicine peddler

doing among the cotton bales? He had expected to find Martin, not the travelling salesman.

Slocum watched around a corner as Poindexter pulled out a knife and stuck it into a bale. He cut a small gash, then thrust his hand inside and wiggled it around, finally withdrawing it. Slocum saw the slump in the shoulders indicating failure. The man was looking for something. If Slocum couldn't get to Martin and find out what this was all about by beating it from the chief clerk, he might be able to accomplish the same thing just by following the peddler. But where did Poindexter come into this mess? None of it made any sense.

DuPont, the pilot. Martin, the chief clerk. Now Poindexter complicated matters.

Poindexter had moved deeper into the jungle of cotton. Slocum hurried after him—too late.

Poindexter cried out, and the sounds of a struggle came back to Slocum, muffled by the cotton all around. He pulled out his Colt Navy in a smooth motion and ran forward, alert for the danger Poindexter had run afoul of.

He saw nothing of the peddler. Slocum crouched down and worked his way toward the starboard side of the boat. His shoulder brushed a hard protrusion. He jerked around, then relaxed a mite. The peddler's thin-bladed knife stuck in a cotton bale. Slocum pulled it out and slid it through the back of his belt. This way he knew where it was. Nothing bothered him more than the idea of someone picking up the knife and using it on him.

His boot touched a slick spot on the wood. Slocum bent, still cautious. With his left hand he scooped up a small amount of the dampness he found.

"Blood," he muttered. "And fresh. Still not even drying."

Staying in the crouch, Slocum duck-walked from the narrow passage and looked back and forth along the length of the entire boat. He heard nothing but the heavy action of the paddlewheels against the water.

And a peculiar crack-crack-crack noise, as if something

hard were smashing against the paddles.

Slocum rushed to a point near the gaudily painted paddle box where he might look down. His eyes widened in horror when he saw the dark shape being battered against the powerfully turning wheel.

He stripped off his gunbelt and took off his boots. There wasn't time for him to strip further. With the peddler's knife clutched between his teeth, Slocum slipped over the railing and found a slippery handhold on the side of the paddle box. His bare feet finding little purchase, Slocum worked his way across until he was within inches of the savagely beating paddlewheel. It took all his will power to keep from thinking of how quickly he might die if he slipped—or how dead James J. Poindexter might be.

That didn't slow his progress. Slocum turned, jumped, and risked death, catching the outer edge of the paddle box. He slid down until he found a tiny ledge. Toes gripping it, he was able to bend over and grab a handful of shirt. Poindexter remained firmly wedged between paddles and box.

Slocum slipped the knife into his hand and slashed frantically. He felt his strength vanishing faster than he'd thought possible. Keeping a grip on the slime-slippery metal and wood surfaces proved more than he could manage. He cut away much of Poindexter's already torn coat. When the peddler slid toward the churning river, Slocum dropped the knife and made a frantic grab.

He caught the man's arm. For a ghastly, stomach-turning second, Slocum thought it would come off in his hands. The flesh had been stripped away by the paddlewheel. But the arm held; Slocum's grip held. He heaved with all his might, and he tossed the peddler up so that he draped over the deck railing.

Panting harshly, Slocum made his way back to the safety offered by that same railing. For long minutes, it seemed that both he and Poindexter were dead. Then Slocum tumbled over and lay stretched out on the deck, dizzy and panting heavily. He forced himself up and dragged Poindexter off the rail.

"Old man, you're dead." Slocum had seen men blown apart by Minie balls and rotting away from gangrene and half a hundred other hideous ways of dying. Seldom had he seen anything this awful. Most of Poindexter's face had been turned to mush by the paddlewheel. His left side was bloody where broken bones protruded through the gray flesh.

Someone had hated the man a great deal to do this to him. Slocum had killed too many men in his day, and had got too many nightmares from killing them, but he could truthfully say that most of the deaths had been clean. A quick, well-aimed bullet, a savage knife slash, but the deaths hadn't been intentionally lingering.

Slocum wondered how long Poindexter had remained aware of his fate. Even a handful of seconds would have been too many. The time from the sounds of struggle to finding the body had been less than a minute.

A minute of being battered by the wheel. Unbridled fear. Helpless panic. Slocum shuddered at the thought. Looking away, he put on his boots, not caring that he dripped water into them. His clothing was ruined, but that seemed little enough to lose compared with what James J. Poindexter, peddler of worthless potions and patent medicines, had lost.

Or was Poindexter more than just a travelling salesman? He had sought something among the bales of cotton, and had done it in a most secretive manner. Slocum had seen the man's stark disappointment when he failed to find it. Had Poindexter been in cahoots with duPont and Martin?

The Colt Navy came to hand as Slocum once again entered the muffled world of the cotton bales. He systematically searched and failed to find anything to explain all he'd witnessed. Disgusted, Slocum returned to where he had left Poindexter's body.

He looked around, at first mistrusting his memory. The small damp spots on the deck—and the blood—convinced him he was not mistaken. Poindexter's body had been removed. Unless Slocum missed his guess, the body had been tossed over the side and claimed by the rolling Mississippi River. No one this side of heaven would see the peddler again.

Squishing in his wet boots, Slocum hurried up to the passenger level. He hesitated, entering the posh ballroom. Although the band had stopped playing many hours earlier, Slocum knew that the gamblers probably still plied their trade. Only when the first light of dawn poked dim rays down through the ballroom skylights would they turn in, to emerge again when the sun dipped low on the horizon. They lived more like moles than humans, spurning the sunlight and living for the night, but Slocum had to admit an affinity with them. Given the chance, he would join their ranks.

But now he had more pressing matters to attend to. Slocum pushed open one of the ornate doors and slipped into the ballroom. Whether it had been the run-in with the river pirates or something else, all the passengers had turned in this night. The huge room stretched the length of the boat, dark and deserted.

This suited Slocum just fine. He went directly to his cabin, intending to change his clothes before exploring further. Poindexter's cabin was several doors down from his. Slocum figured to find some small clue in the man's belongings to explain what was going on.

The Colt slid free in one quick move when he saw the movement on his bed.

"John?" came Eleanore's sleepy voice. "Where have you been? I waited for you. Didn't think Mrs. Hortense would ever go to sleep. Upset by all the excitement, she said. I gave her four drops of laudanum."

"Eleanore, have you seen Poindexter tonight?" Slocum asked.

"What?" The woman stirred restlessly, then pushed to a sitting position. Slocum was all too aware that she was nude under the thin muslin sheet.

"The patent medicine peddler. James J. Poindexter."

"Him? Yes, I saw him. Why? John, what's going on? We aren't in any more danger from the pirates, are we?"

Slocum stripped off his wet clothes and used a towel to dry himself. Eleanore slid across the large bed and complicated matters, her eager fingers seeking out places he'd as soon she not touch.

"John, you are coming to bed?" she asked. "I went through hell getting Mrs. Hortense to sleep. I'm not going to waste all that effort. And," she said, her voice turning even sexier, "any effort we make together is *so* nice."

"Got to go for a few minutes, then I'll be back," Slocum said.

"Promise?" She sounded as if she pouted. Slocum turned and kissed her lips. They were lush, full, damp from the passionate woman's tongue lightly touching them.

"Yes."

"John, where are you going?" Eleanore sounded as if she'd just fully awakened and realized what he'd said.

"Tell you when I get back." Slocum quickly ducked back into the ballroom, went the few doors down to Poindexter's stateroom, and lightly jiggled the door. Locked. But this didn't present any great barrier for Slocum. He was determined to finish off what he had started and find out about Poindexter's involvement in this crazy affair.

A hard shoulder applied to the door caused the flimsy lock to snap. Slocum staggered into the room, clinging to the door handle for balance. He closed the door, noting that it wouldn't latch properly now. Eyes adapting to the dark, Slocum began going through the fancy carved cherrywood armoire holding Poindexter's clothes. The man travelled light: a change of underwear and nothing else.

In Poindexter's bags Slocum found a dozen different bottles filled with variously colored fluids. He sniffed at several and recognized various scents as river water, chicory, cinnamon, but found himself at a loss to identify the rest.

Not what I'm looking for, he thought in disgust. He

continued searching through the bags and found nothing but the labels and empty bottles for the patent medicines Poindexter sold.

In the narrow clothes wardrobe Slocum found Poindexter's spare shirt and coat.

"Poor bastard won't need these now," he said. He reached out and lightly ran his finger down the tattered coat lapel. He jerked his hand back when something sharp pricked his finger.

Slocum gingerly reached out and took the well-worn broadcloth coat from its wooden hanger. Frowning, he studied the lapel. Fastened under it he found a metal button. Turning it around, holding it up so that the dim light within the cabin reflected off it, Slocum painstakingly read the inscription: United States Treasury.

Poindexter had been a Yankee lawman.

Slocum felt no sympathy for the man. He had no love for the Yankees to begin with. Too much had happened in the South during Reconstruction for Slocum to embrace them with open arms. And this Poindexter had been a lawman. The federal marshals tracked down Slocum no matter where he went. Maybe this Treasury agent posing as a patent-medicine had picked up the scent.

Slocum shook his head. That didn't set well with the facts. Poindexter had shown no interest at all in him, even after it became widely known that Sam Jackson had been murdered and Slocum had been deeded the *Excalibur*.

"Poindexter knew I didn't kill Jackson, and the only way he could have known that was if he had the goods on someone else," Slocum mused. Slocum didn't need to be much of a gambler to give even odds on Alexander duPont and Leander Martin being the ones involved with the U. S. Treasury.

Slocum heaved a deep sigh. Instead of finding the single clue that would clear everything up, all he had done was to make the waters even muddier. The harder he tried, the more complicated things got. And Slocum was getting damned tired of it. Martin and duPont—and Slocum had to consider the New Orleans attorney Berton Fellows as being linked to all that had happened—had been involved in something that had interested the Treasury agent.

But what?

"Bales of cotton, sure," he snorted. There had to be more. Something hidden within the bales, or one of the bales, provided the key to Sam Jackson's death, Poindexter's death, and all the rest.

Slocum felt tireder than he had in weeks. Drained, he returned to his cabin, almost reluctant to face the eager, amorous Eleanore Dahlquist.

10

Slocum returned to his stateroom and found Eleanore waiting for him. He dropped onto the bed beside her. The woman's soft brown eyes widened when he silently showed her the U. S. Treasury badge that had been pinned to the inner lapel of James J. Poindexter's spare coat.

"John, this means..." The words trailed off as she covered her mouth with her hand.

"It means we got a world of trouble heading our way," Slocum said, his voice low. "He must have been nosing around trying to find whatever it was that Sam Jackson was smuggling." Slocum slammed his fist down hard into the bed and muttered, "I wish I knew what it was."

"It must be important and very valuable, John," Eleanore said quietly. Her hands stroked over his arms, found the bulges of his biceps, made tiny circling motions on the hair matting his sinewy forearms. "We might be rich if you found whatever it was."

"We?" Slocum said, amused. "Whatever it is, Martin

and the others are willing to kill for it." He leaned back on the soft bed, letting the feather mattress shape itself to his broad shoulders and strong back. Slocum felt as if he floated, separated from the world. Everything had become so unreal he hardly knew what happened any longer. He might have been more tired at some time in his life, but Slocum couldn't say exactly when. He worked leaden arms and legs and began to relax and think on his life for the past week since inheriting the *Excalibur*.

Sam Jackson had come back into his life and had gone almost as swiftly. The *Excalibur* was a fine riverboat and Sean O'Malley was the man to captain her, but Slocum knew he was out of his league as owner. He heaved a sigh and wished he could somehow transport them instantly upriver to St. Louis. He'd been shot up, the *Excalibur* had fended off a pirate attack and been grounded on a sandbar, men had died—killing a Yankee lawman meant only big trouble ahead—and Slocum was tired to the bones of it all. He wanted to turn the *Excalibur* over to Marie Jackson, get a horse, and get off the Mississippi and back to the mountains and prairies he knew. Slocum had the gut feeling that if he stayed too much longer on the river, he'd end up like Sam Jackson and James Poindexter.

"We're partners, aren't we, John?" Eleanore Dahlquist cooed. She licked his ear, dipped her tongue into the hollow cavity beneath it, and breathed hotly. He responded, even though he wasn't much in the mood. The man wanted nothing more than to sleep for a while and pretend that his troubles were all gone.

Eleanore had other ideas.

"We can take Mr. Fellows's offer and accept the agent's commission for transferring the title of the boat," Eleanore said. "I'm sure Mrs. Jackson doesn't want to own a riverboat. Think of the trouble! And, from all you've told me of her, she didn't want Sam going out on the river, anyway. She refused to go with him." Eleanore nibbled lightly at Slocum's earlobe. "She was a fool not to follow her man.

I'd go anywhere . . . with the right man."

Eleanore left little to the imagination. Slocum knew what she meant. She considered the two of them a team, a partnership. And Slocum had to admit the idea didn't strike him as all that bad. Eleanore Dahlquist was a lovely woman, demure in public and totally wanton once they were in bed.

He could do a lot worse, and had in the past. Still, Slocum wasn't about to let her tie him down. He had places to see, and having a fine woman like Eleanore along wasn't going to make it easy. She'd hate the trail life. What would she think the first time they were trapped out in the middle of Iowa and a blue norther came shrieking down from Canada? That was no kind of life for a woman. From the way Eleanore spoke, she intended for him to get the money out of the *Excalibur* and settle down.

Big cities made Slocum uneasy—not only because the chance of being spotted by a federal marshal increased, but because there were too many people crowding in, jostling his elbow, rankling with their continual chatter. He didn't mind company now and again, but to be surrounded by people all the time? That wasn't any kind of life for John Slocum.

"This contraband Captain Jackson talked about. What do you think it is?" Eleanore moved closer to him, her body stroking up and down like a contented feline. She actually purred as she wrapped her sleek, strong white thighs around Slocum's upper leg and began gently rocking to and fro. He felt her wetness through his trouser leg.

"Can't rightly say. I'm finding it harder and harder to think about it," he said truthfully. The sight of her breasts nakedly bobbing about distracted him. The dark nipples visibly stiffened with desire as Eleanore rubbed herself harder against him.

He gasped when her hand dropped between his legs and pressed hard into the bulge she found there. "I'm finding it harder and harder, too," she said in a husky whisper.

Slocum knew there wasn't any other answer than to turn

to her. Their lips met. The kiss started passionate and deep-ened as their desires rose and took total control of their senses. Slocum found himself lost in the feathery caresses, the gentle blowings, the hard kisses, the warm closeness Eleanore provided.

"You make me feel like I'm the only woman in the world." Her fingers worked to get his shirt off. The gunbelt went next. Eleanore's fingers lingered on the hard metal barrel of the Colt Navy, then returned to tear at his trousers feverishly. She had him naked in the bed next to her before Slocum really knew what was happening. And that was fine with him.

He needed the release the lovely brunette promised him. Too much had happened too quickly. He had not had a chance to step back and just think about what it all meant. He'd been too caught up in murder and intrigue to figure out what he ought to do. With Eleanore, those decisions could be put away and forgotten for the time being. The decisions he had to make with the woman were easy, ex-citing, right.

He kissed her ruby lips, tasted the sweetness of her mouth, and moved lower. Eleanore urged him on, her hands strok-ing and guiding.

"Yes, John, do it. Oh, it's so good when you do that!"

He sucked at one nipple, kissed it, and moved to the other. He felt the nubbins of flesh hardening even more under his oral caresses. And Eleanore pressed herself even more fervently against him, if that were possible.

His fingers stroked over the smooth curves of her behind and lifted her off the bed. Her thighs parted in obvious invitation.

"It's time, John. I need you so. Don't make me wait. Please, oh, *oh!*"

He rolled atop her and moved into the vee formed by her legs. With a smooth motion he slipped forward, and the tip of his erection brushed across her lust-dampened nether lips. Eleanore reached between them and took his manhood firmly in hand. She stroked up and down a few quick times, then tugged insistently. He followed her silent instruction. The head of his iron-hard length sank into her willing flesh.

A shudder passed through her entire body. She closed her eyes and let out a gasp. Fingers clutching at his back, she urged him on—as if he needed it. Feeling her womanly sheath all about him, gripping warmly and wetly, caused instinctive reactions in his body. Slocum wasn't even aware of the slow move forward, but the ages-old rhythm he began drove them both wild with pleasure.

He burned for the way Eleanore moved around him. Her fingers raking his back, her legs locked around his waist, her hips lifting off the bed to meet his incoming thrusts, the circular grinding once he was buried to the hilt. Their needs blazed within them as their movements became as one.

"John, oh, yes, John. YES!"

The woman's body arched up as desire quaked through her. Every muscle locked, then released. He kept up his movements, faster now, seeking the release Eleanore had already received. And Slocum got it. The burning tide of passion rose white-hot within him, and he spilled his seed within her hungering cavity. She clung to him with liquid tenacity, and only after he had begun to turn flaccid did Eleanore relax.

"It's good between us, John. So damn good. It's been a long time since I found a man who made me feel the way you make me feel."

"How's that?" He lay back while Eleanore's fingers idly played in the thick mat of dark hair on his chest. She traced out tiny patterns, then pulled the sweat-damp hair up into tiny spirals before kissing them back flat.

"You make me feel like a woman again. When I'm with Mrs. Hortense, it's like I'm nothing more than a child, a mere baby. She tells me what to do and treats me as if I were six years old again."

"You're one hell of a sexy six-year-old," he said, smiling.

"John, be serious." She thwacked him with her open hand. He hardly felt it. "Even with my husband, rest his soul, it was never like this."

Slocum tried to think of all the problems facing him. Leander Martin figured right at the top of the heap. Slocum knew the scrawny chief clerk was mixed up in all the killings right up to his jug ears. Overhearing the conversations with the roustabout and Berton Fellows confirmed this. But Eleanore kept Slocum from working out a good way of taking care of Martin. He didn't want to shoot the man or throw him over the side of the riverboat, much as the chief clerk had done to James Poindexter, but Slocum wasn't going to overlook this as a possibility. There was a definite appeal to the idea of just lynching the clerk, but this created new problems—ones more dangerous to Slocum. He didn't want the law nosing around, asking too many questions. They might find out about his past.

What Slocum wanted more than anything else was a way of directing the law toward Leander Martin without drawing attention to himself. That dead carpetbagger judge in Georgia still filled his sleep with nightmares and his days with bounty hunters waving wanted posters offering some paltry reward for his hide.

"John, what are you planning to do after you get to St. Louis?"

"Hadn't given it much thought," he said. Slocum turned and looked at the brunette lying beside him. She looked like an angel now, the soft brown hair haloing her lovely face, the bedsheets lightly draped over her naked body. But she had been more like a devil a few minutes earlier. Slocum had seldom found a woman with her fire or insatiable needs.

"I don't want to stay with Mrs. Hortense."

Slocum had figured this out for himself. The portly woman was a petty tyrant and nowhere near the kind of companion a vital woman like Eleanore Dahlquist needed. Eleanore ought to be able to support herself at any number of jobs other than nursemaiding an old woman overly intent on her aches and pains and vapors. But Slocum wasn't sure if he wanted to be the answer to Eleanore's escape. He saw all too clearly what she was leading up to and he didn't want to talk about it now, not with killers running around loose on the *Excalibur*.

"The kind of life I lead isn't for you, Eleanore," he said slowly, choosing the words carefully so as not to offend her. "You deserve more. A fine house, all the best. I can't promise anything like that."

"If you're there, it wouldn't matter, John."

"It would," he insisted. "You don't know anything about me. You think I must be some kind of rich tycoon because I happen to be the owner of the *Excalibur* right now."

"You explained all that." Her fingers ran lightly over his chest, his belly, lower. He was exhausted from all that had happened, but somehow he couldn't push that slender-fingered hand away. It felt too damn good, and having Eleanore beside him meant too damn much right now. He had been alone most of the time since the War—and even during it.

Slocum had made few friends among the soldiers and even fewer among Quantrill's band. He had fit in by not being different, but that didn't mean he had to like the men he fought alongside. That had caused the final blowup between them. He had been terribly alone recovering from his wounds, without family or friends. Drifting hadn't allowed bonds to form, either. Slocum guessed this was one reason he took Sam Jackson's death so hard.

Sam represented a past, a happier past in Calhoun County. Sam had been a reminder that normal life was possible—and then that illusion shattered when the bushwhackers shotgunned him. More than anything else, Slocum had decided to take the *Excalibur* north to Marie Jackson and turn it over to her for the sake of that fleeting sensation of friendship, the hint of times past when he was able to stay in one place and put down roots.

"You know I'm running from the law."

"John," Eleanore said earnestly, "it doesn't matter. Not to me. Whatever they want you for, it couldn't be bad. You're not an evil man. I know. You're kind and good . . . and good to me." Her fingers closed around him and began stroking slowly, in ways designed to get him hard again quickly.

Slocum took her wrist and stopped the movement. His eyelids drooped and sleep was only a few minutes away. He needed the shuteye more than he needed another passionate wrestling match with Eleanor.

"We can talk about what we're going to do later. Right now I want to sleep."

"You men. You're all alike. I'm worried, John. Mrs. Hortense might fire me before we get to St. Louis."

"Because you're associating with low-lifes like me?" He had to laugh at this. Eleanore's employer had such delicate sensitivities, or so she'd like everyone to believe.

"She's in no position to say anything about that. Not with the company she kept tonight."

Slocum frowned. He thought the young woman meant Captain O'Malley, but Slocum knew he stood watch with the assistant pilot Smithson.

"Who are you talking about?"

"This is what I've wanted to tell you, but you've kept me from it. Mrs. Hortense has been seeing that chief clerk, Leander Martin."

Slocum sat up in the bed and stared at the woman. She smiled broadly, happy that she had given him such a start. Eleanore seemed to be saying that she could give Slocum more than a good time in bed, that she was useful to him in other ways.

"How much company is she keeping with him?" Slocum asked.

"More than I would have thought." Eleanore almost smirked now at the idea of her snooty employer with a mere riverboat shipping clerk, who smelled of fish and the Mississippi mud.

Slocum's mind raced, piecing together possibilities. He didn't like any of the answers he got back. Depending on how much company Mrs. Hortense had kept with Martin, this might put a new light on Poindexter's murder. It might not have been Martin who was responsible. Then Slocum shook his head, clearing it of the muzzy haze fatigue had dropped over his brain. While Martin might not have been the one who shoved the Treasury agent over the side of the boat and into the paddlewheels, he was still mixed up in it. The roustabout could have done it, or even Alexander duPont. The pilot had nothing to do since Smithson and O'Malley started standing watches to reduce his time in the pilot house.

Martin might not have murdered by his own hand, but he knew who had, and he had given the order ... or had received the order to kill Poindexter.

"She can be such a bitch," said Eleanore. "I'm quite sure she is capable of dismissing me without a fare-thee-well. I wouldn't put it past her to fire me without even a penny of severance pay."

"Not without having someone else to look after her," said Slocum. He wondered if Mrs. Hortense might not be seeking that in Leander Martin. The clerk offered a bit of excitement in what had to be a dull life for the woman. Her husband's illness left her more vulnerable than she might be otherwise, and the lure of whatever contraband was stashed aboard the *Excalibur* could draw any but the most honest.

Slocum snorted. He was anything but honest himself, not considering it anything but fortunate when a bank or a train presented itself bloated with money for his taking, but before he could decide how best to use whatever was being smuggled, he had to locate it—or at least find out what it was everyone was so eager to get.

Fellows had placed a minimum of eighteen thousand dollars on it. What was the most it was worth?

"We are made for one another, John," Eleanore said. "Say you'll take me with you, wherever you go after we get to St. Louis. Say it. Please?"

"Have you ever met Mr. Hortense?"

"What? No, of course not. I've never been farther north than Baton Rouge. Mrs. Hortense hired me almost the same day I got into New Orleans." Eleanore looked at him as if he had sprouted horns.

"John, what's wrong?" the young woman said. "Mrs. Hortense hired me. Mr. Hortense was ill and she needed me to accompany her home. I knew it was odd, but she made it sound perfectly commonplace behavior."

"It's nothing," Slocum said. "I just went off on a side trail."

"John," Eleanore said, returning to what mattered most to her, "when we finally get to St. Louis, will you let me stay with you?"

"We're a week or more out of St. Louis. Let's enjoy the time while we can. Whatever happens when we arrive, there won't be luxury like this."

"You're the only luxury I need," she said, snuggling closer, her hand returning to its feverish movement. Slocum sighed. Eleanore was bound and determined to make herself indispensible to him. Her need for someone to look after her was great, and Slocum wasn't really sure he wasn't the one to do it. That bothered him. He considered himself a loner. Slocum responded to the woman's gentle suasions.

Eleanore Dahlquist proved very convincing that she would never disappoint him.

Just as they were finishing again and Slocum slowly succumbed to the heavy waves of tiredness, the *Excalibur* shuddered deeply, shaking all the way down to her beam. Eleanore curled up next to him, already breathing softly, quietly asleep. Slocum tried to remember what it had felt like when duPont had grounded the boat.

This was a different sensation, different and much more frightening. A bass rumbling passed through the riverboat's timbers like a riverbound earthquake trying to start. Slocum lay awake, waiting for the other shoe to drop. When it didn't come, he put it off to the mind-numbing fatigue clutching at his senses.

The shudder came again, deeper, more threatening.

He sat bolt upright in bed, awakening Eleanore. She blinked dewy eyes at him. Soft fingers reached for him, seeking comfort and reassurances that everything was all right. Before she could speak, the *Excalibur* shook all over. The explosion and resulting roar sent Slocum rocketing from the bed and grabbing for his trousers. Whatever mischief Martin and duPont and their cohorts were up to now sounded bad.

And deadly for everyone aboard the riverboat.

11

Slocum raced from his stateroom, ignoring Eleanore's cries for him to stop. The bone-shaking roar he heard spurred him on. Whatever caused it threatened the entire riverboat. Slocum skidded to a halt on the walkway outside and peered down at the boiler deck. Flames licked along the edges of the *Excalibur* and were starting to rise up level with his eyes. That meant tongues of fire over twenty feet high.

In spite of the heat boiling up and blistering his face, Slocum went cold inside.

Visions of the *Excalibur* engulfed in flame came to him. In the middle of the river they would look like a drawing he had seen once of an old Viking funeral pyre. The Viking ship had been laden with the dead warrior's body and then cast adrift on the sea, set afire. Slocum shuddered at the idea of dying by either burning or drowning.

He swung around and raced down the stairs. Beneath his feet the riverboat shuddered and shook with new vibrations, tremors even more disturbing than the one when the boiler had erupted in all directions.

Sean O'Malley had beaten him to the boiler deck. The captain wended his way through the tall stacks of cordwood and stood as close to the destroyed boiler as possible. Chief Engineer Macallum talked with him, arms waving. Slocum saw that the engineer was arguing with the captain.

". . . I tell ya, Cap'n, it was the goddamn rivets we got from that Frog mechanic in New Orleans. Bad, they were. The rivets popped when they got too hot and the whole damn boiler went up." Macallum pointed at the results.

"Mr. Macallum," Slocum asked, "is there any chance that this may have been something other than an accident?"

The man shook his head. The dancing light from the fire burning on the deck gave him a curiously demonic aspect. The engineer snorted derisively before answering.

"That Frog don't know enough to do it wrong on purpose," Macallum said. "He gave us shoddy material, nothing more. Damn his eyes!"

O'Malley took Slocum aside and let Macallum tend to the fire. Slocum eyed it suspiciously. It spread with horrifying rapidity, edging toward the stacks of wood all around. The boiler itself had been encased in firebrick, but when the seams ruptured, the brick had been blown free, exposing the ranks of wood to the flames. The deck itself had been eaten through by the fire, and the cams and pistons were in danger of being warped from the intense heat generated.

"Let him be, Mr. Slocum," said Captain O'Malley. "The man's got worries enough without you asking fool questions and distracting him."

"Just trying to figure out if we have more problems than just this," said Slocum. The heat brought out a patina of greasy sweat on Slocum's forehead. Being this near raging death made him uneasy, but if O'Malley didn't flinch away from it, he wouldn't.

"We do," the captain said firmly, "but we must address them later. I will personally rip the arms off this ironmonger for supplying inferior rivets." The captain turned his pale eyes toward the destroyed boiler. "That would make an adequate coffin for the thieving Frenchman."

Slocum considered the possibilities and decided that this must be an unfortunate accident. If any contraband was stashed aboard the *Excalibur*, it would surely burn to cinders or go to the bottom of the Mississippi if the riverboat sank. No one gained that way.

The man went cold thinking of another possible reason for the boiler explosion. There might be more than one group interested in Sam Jackson's hidden illicit merchandise. One group might be trying to find it—Martin and duPont and the lawyer Fellows—and another might be attempting to destroy it. Slocum sighed when he realized that the government lawmen also sought the road to Sam's riches.

Letting the *Excalibur* burn to the waterline might be the best thing for him. Attention would focus on the destruction of the boat, and he could slip off into the night. He had a pocketful of Yankee greenbacks from his gambling successes. What little more he could get from the petty cash funds aboard the *Excalibur* might keep him in tucker and horses and women and whiskey for many months.

"No!" he shouted, slamming his fist against a four-foot length of cordwood. "I won't give in that easy."

O'Malley looked at him oddly but said nothing. Slocum wasn't a quitter, never had been and never would be. He wasn't going to turn tail and run simply because the game played harder than he'd thought it might.

"They aren't getting the fire under control fast enough. Want to see us go to the bottom?" he demanded.

O'Malley smiled and held out his hand, indicating Slocum might want to give a hand at the pumps pulling the filthy water from the river and squirting it onto the orange tongues of fire. Slocum said nothing, but joined the roustabouts working the pump handle up and down. Erasmus Washington worked on the other side of the pump. His eyes widened when he saw Slocum, then the man grinned. His muscles rippled, coated with sweat, shining in the bright light cast by the fire. Washington smiled, white teeth showing brilliantly in his black face.

Between him and Slocum, they kept the pump sucking water long enough to control the worst of the fire. By the time both men were ready to collapse from exhaustion, Macallum had the "doctor" steam engine switched about. The tiny engine began doing the job the two of them had—and better. A steady stream of water rose from the river and spewed forth onto the fire. In less than fifteen minutes after the steam engine began pumping, the fire had been put out.

Slocum stood next to O'Malley and stared. The decking had been turned to charcoal and the boiler itself was blackened beyond recognition. But Macallum seemed satisfied. He moved through the filth and blackness, sloshing in puddles of yellow-black water, callused hands stroking over the hot metal as if it were a new lover's flesh.

"The boiler is unhurt, except for the popped rivets," Macallum called up.

"How can he say that?" Slocum muttered. "The boiler's entire side is blown free. It'll take months to repair it. Might as well throw the entire thing into the river."

O'Malley laughed at this. "You have no faith in Mr. Macallum. If he says it's unhurt, then he can fix it and he will fix it. I have known the engineer only a short while, but the bloody damned Scotsman knows his work well."

Slocum was dubious. The destruction looked to be too extensive for anything but scraping.

"Mr. Slocum, go back to your bed and rest—or whatever else you might find there to do. We will take care of this. It is, after all, our job, and one for which you will pay us well in bonuses."

"You old river pirate," Slocum growled. He slapped the captain on the back and went up to the cargo deck. He looked at the burned area on the boiler deck and shook his head. They would have to put into a port for repairs. He saw no way around it. The *Excalibur* ran on only one engine. While seven boilers remained, the engine on the port side was inoperative because of the damage done to the pistons on the engine itself. Slocum could hardly believe the size of those boilers: thirty-two feet long and near four feet in diameter. The destruction caused by one of them blowing apart had been awesome.

He thanked his lucky stars that the damage had been ruled minor by Macallum and O'Malley. Slocum had no desire to see what they might consider major damage.

Slocum tiredly climbed the stairs to the upper walkway where the passengers huddled together. The preacher—Duggan by name, if Slocum remembered aright—struck a pose and cried, "The vengeance of the Lord is brought upon this wicked vessel. He shall smite it with his fiery sword as he smote Sodom and Gomorrah!"

Slocum glanced to the railing and the decks below and considered throwing Duggan over. Let his Lord save him. Then Slocum got control of his temper. He outshouted the hellfire-and-brimstone preacher. "Please! Go back to your cabins. The captain has everything under control. There is no danger."

"But the fire..." someone said in a quavering voice. "We're going to sink."

"Only one boiler developed any trouble," Slocum said. "There are seven more. And the fire is out. Go back to bed. There's nothing to worry about."

Slocum saw Eleanore Dahlquist looking out of his stateroom. He flashed her a reassuring smile and was surprised when she didn't look in the least comforted by it. As Slocum went to his cabin, he passed by one of the full-length mirrors dotting the walls of the ballroom. He had to laugh at the horrible figure reflected back. His clothing had been turned soot-black. The buttons on his coat had actually melted and tiny holes had burned from flying embers sticking to the fabric. His face looked more like Erasmus Washington's than that of a gentleman farmer from Calhoun County, Georgia, and he left behind a trail of charcoal wherever he walked.

"John," the woman said, obviously worried, "are you all

right? You look such a mess." She backed away from him when he reached out to touch her cheek.

"You certainly are the one with compliments tonight. Just what a man needs to hear." Slocum heaved a deep breath. "A bath. Get a steward to draw me a bath. The owner of the *Excalibur* must have some privileges."

"Yes, John." Eleanore slipped out. Slocum sighed. From the tone of her voice, he wouldn't see the brunette again that night. He rubbed one hand across his sweaty forehead. The hand came away even blacker than it had been before. Slocum looked in the mirror on the back of the door and shook his head.

"You, John Slocum, are one hell of a mess." His eyebrows had been singed and his hair was in disarray, reminding him of a wild man he had seen in a travelling carnival as a child. Slocum winced as he moved to strip off his shirt and coat. His muscles ached from the vigorous work he had done on the water pump. By the time the steward had drawn him a bath, Slocum didn't even care that the water was only tepid. He sank into the tin tub and let the water work at the soot covering him.

Afterward, he didn't mind that Eleanore had returned to her own cabin. He needed sleep, and she would have kept him from it. Pleasurably, true, but he needed rest more than he did the lovely brunette's enticing nearness. Slocum snored loudly within seconds of his head touching the feather pillow.

"Mr. Macallum and I agree that we must put in to a dock to perform the necessary repairs," Captain O'Malley said. "I am reluctant to do so because of the delay it will cause. The cargo and passengers must not be held up longer than a day or two. Already we are behind schedule. Intolerable." The crusty captain paced, hands clasped behind his back. Slocum had the feeling that the only thing worse in the man's eyes than not maintaining the *Excalibur*'s schedule was allowing the boat to sink.

"Have you mentioned this to anyone else?" Slocum asked.

"You refer to Mr. duPont. Yes, son, I had to tell him. Smithson is almost exhausted. He stood back-to-back watches, and these were longer than normal watches, I might add. He is a fine pilot. With more experience Smithson might be one of the best on the river. But he is not made of iron. If a pilot's eyes tire from fatigue, he endangers the entire boat. We must see to it that he is given some rest."

"Putting in to dock," mused Slocum, "might give us the chance to dismiss duPont. Fire him and find a new pilot."

O'Malley shook his head. "We are still below Baton Rouge. Once we pass that fair city, the going is easier. We will have the poplars on the riverbanks to help us navigate. But here?" O'Malley shook his head. "We need a competent pilot, and any looking for work will not be competent."

"All the good ones already have berths. Is that what you're saying?"

"Yes, son, it is."

Slocum thought hard on what duPont and Martin might be up to. They knew of the *Excalibur*'s condition and O'Malley's decision to put in to a dock for repairs. His hand rested lightly on the ebony butt of his Colt Navy. The boiler explosion had been only the first round in what might prove to be a real battle. Accidental or not, it had injured four men Slocum counted on in a real fight; all four of the firemen had been hired by Sam Jackson and, as such, Slocum considered them to be allies.

"How long before we find a dock?"

"In this part of the river, not longer'n a few hours. I've told Smithson and duPont to reduce speed and steam at no more than quarter. I do not want the one good engine damaged also. We'd be in this godforsaken stretch of river for the rest of our days."

Slocum hoped that O'Malley wasn't the prophet the preacher Duggan claimed to be.

* * *

"There," said O'Malley, pointing. "Put the *Excalibur* in to that dock, Mr. duPont."

The pilot glowered, then tugged at the jingler to signal the engineer for reduced power. Maneuvering the *Excalibur* proved even trickier than usual due to the paddlewheel on the port side being shut down. But duPont was skilled and they docked without mishap. Slocum had held his breath for the last few feet, but the pilot's ability was such that they hardly banged into the pilings. The deckhands jumped to the dock and lashed the boat securely.

"I had best see to finding a skilled ironworker. That might be as hard as . . ." O'Malley let the sentence trail off. Slocum understood the captain's meaning. Finding men able to repair the boiler might be as hard as getting another pilot.

DuPont seemed to sense the meaning, also. His usual sarcastic tones were even more pronounced when he spoke. "Is there anything else the captain wants?" he asked.

"A civil tongue in your head," snapped O'Malley, "but I know that's asking too much."

DuPont left the pilot house without another word. Slocum had bad feelings about the man. And Slocum wished he had found the time to confront Martin about Poindexter's murder. But there had been so little time that wasn't filled with one calamity or another. Fire and burst boilers. Killings. The need to discover Sam Jackson's contraband—both what it was and where it had been hidden.

Slocum rode on a bomb waiting to go off, and he didn't know how to defuse it without creating a bigger explosion.

"Mistuh Slocum, kin I have a word with you?" asked Erasmus Washington. The roustabout glanced nervously over his shoulder, as if expecting someone to interrupt.

"What is it, Ras?"

"Why we told to unload the cotton bales on the port side? They's not in the way of repairing the boiler."

"Unload?" Slocum frowned. "Who gave the order?"

"Mistuh Martin did. He said he was told to do it by that

pilot, duPont. The one with shifty eyes and fancy moustache."

Slocum leaned over the railing and saw the scrawny, pock-faced chief clerk pointing out the bales the roustabouts were about to move. The steam-powered crane had been swung around and hooks attached to lift the bales onto the dock.

"Tell them to wait until the captain can speak to them, Ras." Slocum hurried back up to the pilot house where O'Malley and Smithson were going over charts of the river to determine the next leg of their trip after the boiler was fixed.

"Captain," said Slocum, "I'd like a word with you."

"We are engaged in making important decisions, Mr. Slocum. Please return later."

"Why is the cargo being unloaded?" Slocum demanded.

"What are you talking about?"

"Go look. DuPont ordered the cotton bales on the port side, forward of the boiler, to be taken off. So they can repair the boat, they said."

"Impossible. Pilots don't give orders when in port. Only the captain can do that." O'Malley stalked to the front of the hurricane deck and peered below. The bellow emanating from his throat rocked Slocum back.

"That rapscallion!" O'Malley raged, storming back to the pilot house. "How dare duPont give orders to unload cargo? How dare Martin obey!"

O'Malley's anger raged. He slammed his fist down on the charts he and Smithson had been studying and then reached for a shotgun he had taken from Sam Jackson's rack in the captain's office. Slocum started to say something, then bit back the words. O'Malley realized this might be the showdown. Slocum hitched up his gunbelt and wished he had brought along his second Colt. His fingers drummed on the butt, then he nodded to O'Malley.

"Mr. Smithson," Sean O'Malley told the young pilot,

"stay here. If anything happens to me, the *Excalibur* is yours to command."

"But, sir, you can't go down there alone!"

A mirthless smile crossed the old man's lips. He tilted his head toward Slocum and said, "With him beside me, how can you say I'm going alone, eh?"

"Sorry, sir." Smithson's expression told the story. Slocum's stance, the way he held his face coldly impassive, showed his determination. Slocum almost laughed at the young pilot. He had it written all over him that he'd never call out Slocum and thought anyone who would a fool.

But then Slocum knew very well how he looked before a fight.

"Let's not stand about waiting for the steward to serve tea," said O'Malley. "This has gone too far. A clerk and a goddamn *pilot* giving orders in port. Impossible!"

"How many of the crew will duPont and Martin have on their side?" asked Slocum. "I figure we're up against at least ten, maybe twice that."

"What are you saying, son? A crew is loyal to the captain—or else!"

"You forget the roustabouts hired by Martin. You can bet your bottom dollar that they are all in his pay."

"Impossible," said O'Malley in such a way that Slocum knew the captain protested only from years of long habit. He understood all that had happened aboard the *Excalibur:* mutiny. Slocum didn't care how O'Malley rationalized it if they stood a fighting chance of keeping control of the riverboat—and staying alive to brag about it later.

O'Malley jumped the last four steps to the cargo deck, the long-barreled shotgun pointing about in front of him like a bird dog's nose seeking a downed duck. O'Malley motioned to Erasmus Washington and several others standing nearby, quietly talking among themselves.

"Mr. Washington," the captain said, "what is the situation?"

"As I told Mistuh Slocum, they's unloading the cotton

and stacking the bales on the dockside. Didn't want no help. They said they'd do it themselves. Suits me and the others." Washington indicated the seven with him.

"They have no orders to unload any of the *Excalibur*'s cargo. I am assuming this to be an act of mutiny. Do I make myself clear?"

"No, Cap'n, don't rightly think you do." Washington's eyes studied the old man. Slocum saw the questions rising within about O'Malley's ability to stop anyone, much less a large group of determined men headed by the pilot and the clerk.

"You will aid me in quelling this uprising. Mr. Slocum and I require assistance."

"Mistuh Slocum?"

"Can't force you, Ras, but I'd take it as a big favor." Slocum knew the man would help.

Washington looked solemn, scratching his chin with one thick finger. "Think we might get something better'n than grub pile if'n we help out?"

Slocum frowned. He didn't know what the man meant.

O'Malley cut in, "I guarantee fresh food for the remainder of the journey to St. Louis. No more leftovers."

Slocum understood then. All the leftover food from the passengers was given to the roustabouts. This constituted their sole source of tucker.

"Count on it, Ras," Slocum said.

"Good enough for me. Don't mind getting myself kilt if I can get a good meal later on." The powerfully muscled man laughed at this and motioned to the others. Several were skeptical at first, but Ras's huge fist closed under one man's chin. He quickly agreed, but Slocum knew that if gunfire broke out he would be the first to cut and run.

"You, Washington, that way. Don't let them escape." O'Malley pointed to the far side of the riverboat. "Half of you go straight ahead, through the stacks of cargo. Mr. Slocum, come with me."

Slocum walked beside the muttering captain as they went

forward to where the crane swung to and fro, lifting the huge cotton bales and depositing them on the dock. Men sweated in the morning sun while the chief clerk and the pilot went from bale to bale, pointing out which ones to unlead next. There seemed to be no rhyme or reason to the ones they choose. This convinced Slocum that something of great value had been stashed inside the bales. The Treasury agent Poindexter had known that, but he had been unsure which bales.

"Mr. duPont," called out O'Malley, his voice booming like a foghorn, "what is the meaning of this impertinence? You have no authority to order this."

DuPont turned and stared at the captain. He ran slender fingers along his moustaches and pulled the tips up into devil's horns.

"We have a good market for these bales," said duPont. "Profit, old man—that's why we should be in business. There's no profit taking these upriver to St. Louis."

"Stop this immediately." O'Malley punctuated his command with one barrel of buckshot. The roar silenced the men. All that Slocum heard in the void after was the sloshing of river against the sides of the *Excalibur* and the hissing of the steam crane. He stepped to one side and drew his Colt Navy, waiting. If the dozen or more men decided to disobey their captain, the fight could get nasty real fast.

It did.

Leander Martin casually reached into his vest pocket and pulled forth a derringer. He seemed in no hurry, but Slocum was. The .31-caliber slug drove hard into the chief clerk's sternum. The man pitched forward, a surprised look on his face.

Then all hell broke loose.

The roustabouts produced more rusty pistols and brightly gleaming knives than Slocum was willing to face with only five shots left. O'Malley had no such fear. The captain stood his ground.

"I been on the river well nigh forty years," he said.

"There's nothing I haven't seen or faced." He leveled the shotgun as he added, "Or come out on top of."

This slowed the roustabouts for a moment, until duPont yelled at them, "Kill the bastards. Kill them!"

Slocum got off a shot at the pilot and missed. A hail of bullets drove him to cover behind a cotton bale.

O'Malley stood rock-still in the open. "I gave you men an order. Obey it!"

Slocum thought O'Malley would die then and there, but he was startled to see half the roustabouts hesitate. The other eight backed off. O'Malley's voice carried the full power of his years of experience and the arrogance of command.

The spell broke when duPont started firing from the cover of another cotton bale. One bullet hit O'Malley high on the right shoulder. The old man spun about on impact, his finger tensing on the shotgun's trigger. The full load of 00 buck went into the decking.

The hell that O'Malley had postponed erupted anew. And this time the captain lay unmoving on the deck. Slocum emptied his Colt, dropped two of the roustabouts, then started his retreat. Unless he did something fast, duPont would have control of the *Excalibur*.

12

The bullet ripped through the corner of the cotton bale and stung Slocum high on the thigh. He barely noticed. His full attention centered on the roustabout waving the rusty pistol around, firing wildly. The man knew nothing about firearms. He endangered not only Slocum but all those around him.

The gun discharged and another of the roustabouts snarled, swinging at the errant gunman. Slocum took the opportunity to dodge back into the rows of stacked crates and wirebound cotton bales. As he moved, he felt the hot burning streak across his thigh. Limping slightly, he dived flat when he heard a whistling sound.

A prybar crashed into the crate just above his head, but Slocum found himself flat on his belly, unable to escape a second blow.

"You kilt Mr. Martin," the roustabout wielding the prybar said. "I liked him. And he promised me fifty dollars

143

when we got to St. Louis. You robbed me of that money, and I'm gonna kill you for it, you son of a bitch."

The thick iron bar lifted high above the man's head, the full power of mighty shoulders and work-strengthened arms preparing for the stroke downward. Slocum scrambled forward, but his leg failed him at a crucial instant. He looked back over his shoulder and saw triumph on the man's face.

The iron rod began its descent.

Slocum waited to die. When a choked noise reached his ears, he opened his eyes. The roustabout stood as if frozen. The man gaped and fluttered like a trout pulled onto the banks of a stream. Eyes bulging, the roustabout tried to speak, to turn, to move.

Prybar still locked in his hands, he fell forward like a toppled tree. A gleaming baling hook protruded from the center of the man's back.

"Ras!"

"You oughta be more careful, Mistuh Slocum. You can get yourself kilt dead out here."

"It's the company I keep," Slocum said, hoisting himself. He lightly touched the wound on his leg. It tingled and a tiny trickle of blood soaked into his trousers, but he wasn't too badly injured.

Washington pulled the death-giving baling hook out of the fallen man's spine, wiping the tip on the corpse's shirt.

"Never did cotton much to him. He was one of those hired on by Mistuh Martin. Laid about and never done a minute's work. Made it hard on the rest of us."

"They're making it hard on all of us now," said Slocum. A bullet found its way through the labyrinth of crates and sent splinters flying. He motioned to Ras to follow. Keeping low, Slocum wended his way to a central point in the midst of the cargo. Several others joined them there.

"The captain's still out there by the crane," Slocum told them. "I don't know how badly hurt he is, but it didn't look good."

"He's dead," one roustabout said.

"You know that for sure?" Slocum said. He didn't know if any of the others had managed to get close to where O'Malley had fallen.

The man shook his head. "What's the difference? We're all dead if'n we don't get off this boat. It's jinxed, just like they said. You didn't blow the whistle when we passed by a graveyard, and the ghosts are gettin' even with us."

Slocum stood, green eyes as hard and cold as emerald chips. "There's no jinx. Just flesh-and-blood men. Martin's dead. I shot him with this. Does this look like a ghost?" He held up his Colt. The morning sun caught the bluing and sent light scattering off the barrel. "Ghosts don't die. Those are men wanting to kill us. We can fight them."

"They won't fight if'n we leave the boat," the man said, but conviction didn't ring in his words. In the face of Slocum's determination, none of them wanted to argue.

"We get Captain O'Malley first, then we go after the rest of them. The pilot is the one to stop. Get duPont and they'll stop. He's the one keeping them going." Slocum looked around the small group and realized this worked both ways. If duPont killed him, the fight would be over, too. These men weren't interested in dying for nothing—and Slocum couldn't even tell them what the reason for the fight was, because he didn't know.

Sam Jackson's contraband was at the heart of the deadly battle, and he had no idea what it was. Only by going through every last bale of cotton duPont had already unloaded could he find the answer.

Slocum reloaded his Colt and checked what the others carried. Their weapons were as battered and rusty as those used against them. Slocum wished for better, but had to make do with what he had.

"Listen close," he said. "Ras, you take half the men and go up the starboard side of the *Excalibur*. Create a commotion. Lots of noise. Draw their attention."

"And get our fool heads blowed off," grumbled a hulking Cajun roustabout. Washington silenced him with a cuff that sent the man reeling. He slunk back to the tight circle like a whipped cur, but he said nothing more. Slocum wondered if he could be trusted at all. He shrugged it off; that was Washington's worry, not his.

"The rest of us will sneak up and see if we can't pull Captain O'Malley back to the shelter of the bales near the crane."

"Dangerous," said Washington. "But it might work if you don't expect us to stand long again' them."

"I don't. Just a few minutes."

Erasmus Washington nodded. "We can keep them bastards chasin' us long enough."

Slocum watched as Washington and the others with him vanished in the jungle of crates. He went to the port side of the *Excalibur* and looked forward. His Colt came easily to hand and he fired. A roustabout grunted, grabbed at his side, and tumbled into the muddy water. As the riverboat gently swung to and fro on the current, it rolled back toward the dock. The man screamed as the ponderous bulk of the boat caught him and crushed him against a piling. Slocum motioned for the others to follow.

One made a comment about the man turned to bloody mush in the water. Slocum silenced any further talk with an impatient wave of his hand. He wanted duPont's full attention on Erasmus Washington and the men with him.

Slocum sneaked forward, then dropped to his belly. He motioned for those behind him to spread out and cover the trails through the piles of crates. Like a snake, he wriggled toward the steam-powered crane's base and peered around it.

Six men crouched, guns drawn and waiting. With one bullet gone, he had no chance of taking them all out, even if he had wanted to. Slocum spotted Captain O'Malley. The man had been pulled upright and leaned against a heavy wooden crate. He held one arm and glared at his captors.

No easy way of rescuing him existed. While Slocum would never give in to an exchange attempt—O'Malley for the *Excalibur*—he would feel bad if duPont killed the old man.

Slocum signalled to Sean O'Malley. The captain nodded slightly, not drawing any attention to himself or Slocum. Slocum had to smile at this. O'Malley was cagey and knew the ropes. If anyone survived, it would be the old captain. Looking up the side of the crane gave Slocum an idea.

As silent as any Indian, he climbed the girders forming the crane base. When he reached the cross arm that carried the load, he slid out to the very end. One of the men below heard the scrape of leather against metal and looked curiously around, but O'Malley distracted him and got a hard blow to the side of his head for his effort.

O'Malley glowered at the roustabout and said nothing more. The man turned back to his post, sounds of Washington and those with him attracting his attention.

Slocum tugged at the thick hemp cable draped over the end of the crane arm. A hook at the end gave him the chance he needed to rescue O'Malley. Lowering the rope, he motioned for O'Malley to put the hook under his jacket. It took the captain a few seconds to understand Slocum's plan. Then he quickly obeyed, sitting back to wait for what had to come next.

Slocum slithered back down to the base of the crane. The tiny steam engine still chuffed away, forgotten. He stood, got his hands on the crane's controlling levers, and pulled. The giant pulley wheel started to turn as the rope whirled onto the take-up reel.

Sean O'Malley rocketed into the air away from his captors. For a second, none of the men figured out what happened. This gave Slocum the chance to step clear of the crane and fire his five remaining rounds into the tight knot of confused men. Two fell; the other shots missed cleanly.

But the purpose was served. They took cover, distracted by Slocum's shots and the hubbub caused by Erasmus Washington. Slocum swung the crane arm around, then opened the steam safety valve. All power gone in a rush,

O'Malley fluttered to the dockside like a wounded bird. The old man smashed down hard, but he struggled to his feet and scrambled for cover among the cotton bales already unloaded.

He gestured to Slocum showing he was safe, then yelled out, "Get those sons of bitches!"

Slocum ducked behind the crane's base as a fusillade of bullets sought his flesh. He knew better than to stand and fight with an emptied gun. Retreat and live to fight again.

He dropped down and skidded along the splintery decking until he was out of range. By then, Washington and the others had been driven back.

When they rejoined forces, Slocum heard the pilot yelling, "You think you're so smart, Mr. Slocum. I will kill you! I promise you this thing. You will die, Slocum!"

"Sure talks big for such a little man," observed Erasmus Washington.

"He can afford to talk big. He's got what we want." Slocum didn't bother telling Washington that he had no idea what that was. With the captain safe, though, Slocum's choices increased. The worst duPont could do now was to destroy Sam Jackson's contraband. Since Slocum had nothing now, it mattered little if he ended up with nothing. It was the pilot who had everything to lose—and would. Slocum would see to that.

"Ras, keep them on the boat. Don't let them try to jump over to the dock. I'm going to give Mr. duPont and his friends a little entertainment."

"You makes it sound like a giant party," the towering black man said, frowning. "I don't see any fun in this a-tall."

Slocum blinked at the man's words. He *was* getting a perverse enjoyment from this. Not since he had been with Quantrill had he felt this alive. And it frightened him a mite. He had become aware of himself, of the entire world. The slightest noise was heard vividly, the smallest odor or vibration was sensed. His hand held his Colt steadier and he thought faster. He was *alive*.

"It's not," he said. "DuPont will kill any of us if he can. Whatever the stakes are in this game, they're mighty high for him. He's playing for his very life, and we got to do the same."

Slocum hit the stairs leading up to the passenger deck as hard and fast as he could. A few bullets ricocheted off the wood around him, but he reached the walkway safely. A pistol shot at this distance would have to be mighty lucky to hit anything.

A pistol shot.

Slocum intended to use something more accurate for his return fire.

"John, what's happening?" cried Eleanore Dahlquist. He pushed past her and ran for the captain's office without answering. He heard Eleanore's footsteps doggedly following. "John! What is it? There were shots and Mrs. Hortense wanted me to find out if anything was wrong. We aren't being attacked by those awful river pirates again, are we?"

"You might say that," Slocum said, reaching Sam Jackson's gun cabinet. Sharp eyes picked out the best rifle, a .55-caliber Spencer carbine similar to the one he'd stolen off a dead Yankee and used throughout the War. He yanked down the carbine and began stuffing shells into the magazine in the stock. The rest of the box went into the outer pocket of his once-fancy coat. Slocum made himself a promise never again to spend so much money on clothing that would be dirtied and destroyed.

"Tell me, John. I deserve to know!"

The brunette blocked the door, arms crossed just under her ample, heaving breasts, and tapped her foot impatiently. He went to her, took her in his arms, kissed her, then spun her around while she was still gasping. Before Eleanore got her wits about her, he had returned to the walkway on the passenger deck. Slocum got to the stairs and took them three at a time until he reached the hurricane deck in front of the pilot house.

Smithson stood there, pistol in hand.

"Mr. Slocum, is the captain hurt? I saw some of what went on near the crane."

"He'll be all right, if we don't get ourselves killed off by those backshooters," said Slocum. He flopped belly down on the deck and poked the muzzle of the rifle over the edge. The front sight needed a tad of soot on it; the sunlight reflected off the bright bead and made sighting hard, but Slocum had faced worse conditions.

He levered a shell into the chamber, pulled back the heavy hammer on the right side, set the back sights, and waited. The first man who poked his head out from behind a crate got it blown off. The huge Spencer bucked and slammed painfully into Slocum's shoulder, but the message had been properly delivered. He levered in another shell and got another man through the knee as he tried to dive from one side of the *Excalibur* to the other.

"Mr. Slocum," said Smithson, his voice high-pitched with fear, "I've never seen shooting like that."

"I have," Slocum said. The range was less than fifty yards—hardly enough to brag about. He'd sat atop a hill three hundred yards distant in battle and killed blue-coated officers. Slocum had never even seen most of their faces, just reflections off the gold braid.

The carbine blasted again and a third deckhand went spinning into the river, dead.

"DuPont!" Slocum called. "Give it up! You're not going anywhere."

"Don't let the son of a bitch surrender, damn you, Slocum!" came Captain O'Malley's shout from the dock. "I want that mutineer *dead!*"

Slocum fired again, missing his target. Still, even ramming the heavy bullets near the men kept them under cover. This made it easier for Washington and the others to creep up on them. With luck, Washington might even be able to capture a few of duPont's men.

"Slocum," came the pilot's voice from the port side of the riverboat. "We got Macallum and we got control of the engines. All the firemen are under our guns. I call upon you to surrender."

Slocum pictured the gloating, moustached pilot. His blood came to a boil as his hands steadied even more. The next shot found a target: a man's head blew apart like a rotted melon.

"You had your chance, duPont. You should have dealt with me earlier. Now I'm going to do what the captain wants. You're a dead man."

"I'll see the *Excalibur* sunk first," threatened the pilot.

"Smithson!" Slocum called. "Do you see anything over the far edge of the deck? Near the boilers?"

"Yes, sir," the young pilot replied. "It is exactly as Mr. duPont claimed. I see four men holding the engineer and four of the firemen at gunpoint. I...I don't think I can be as accurate as you at this range. I'm not much of a marksman."

"Just fire a bullet or two in duPont's direction. Don't worry about hitting anything." Slocum went to the side and peered over. He took a long, deep, steadying breath. Exhaling hard, he hefted the carbine to his shoulder and fired. The rifle kicked back hard, but not as hard as the man struck by the full force of the bullet.

Slocum jacked in another round, fired, tried for another, and came up empty. Cursing, he dropped to one knee and began reloading, stuffing the cartridges into the butt plate. The spring mechanism almost got away from him, but he finally inserted it and closed the plate, ready for action again.

There was no need. The one shot had thrown duPont's men into disarray. Macallum and the firemen had used the confusion to their advantage, swarming over the mutineers.

When Slocum studied the area around the boilers and engines again, Macallum had regained control. The chief engineer motioned to Slocum that all was well.

Slocum went back to the front of the hurricane deck where Smithson struggled to reload his pistol. The young man's hand shook so badly, he dropped bullets and percussion caps, then made it even worse trying to pick them up again. Many spilled off the edge of the deck and bounced onto the skylights of the ballroom below.

"Stay calm. Imagine you're taking the river north of Baton Rouge," said Slocum.

"But, sir, that's an easy stretch," said the pilot.

"Exactly." Slocum dropped prone again and waited. Even though he had several good shots, he held back. There was only one man he wanted. And when Alexander duPont poked his head up to see what happened as Erasmus Washington advanced, Slocum squeezed back on the Spencer's trigger. The heavy rifle bucked hard and the muzzle lifted. A cloud of black smoke poured from the bore, obscuring Slocum's vision. Only rolling to one side and peering through the slowly dissipating smoke could he see what damage he'd wrought.

The pilot lay flat on his back, not moving. The tips of his moustaches stood out black and gleaming against the whiteness of the dead face. Slocum imagined he saw the tips of that waxed moustache begin to wilt as all life seeped from the body.

"DuPont's dead," Slocum shouted down. "Surrender and you won't be harmed."

"The devil they won't," came O'Malley's aggrieved voice. "They are foul mutineers. They will be executed for this!"

Slocum chuckled. The old man's honor had been sullied. His first command since the War had been marred by what he saw as mutiny. Slocum didn't care what Sean O'Malley said. He wasn't going to gun down those roustabouts surviving this battle. And he didn't have to worry.

One splash after another sounded. The men dived overboard, swimming against the powerful Mississippi current for the safety of land around a bend and out of sight of the *Excalibur*. Slocum counted and saw eight bobbing heads. With the ones dead or wounded, he reckoned this accounted for all those in duPont and Martin's pay.

Slocum sat, feet dangling over the edge of the hurricane deck, watching as Washington and the others made a quick check of the cargo and forward area.

O'Malley strutted out onto the dock, holding his wounded arm. The man might have been the one responsible for driving off the mutineers, so big was the smile on his face.

"Mr. Washington, get those lazy men to work. Reload these bales. I want them lashed down firmly within the hour. And, Mr. Macallum—where the hell is my engineer?"

"Aye, Captain," came the faint answer. "We're hard at work on refitting the boiler."

"Taking you long enough. Can't find good help these days," the captain grumbled. "And someone get a gangplank down. Do you expect me to jump across to my boat?"

Slocum got to his feet. Smithson stood, whey-faced and still shaking. Slocum slapped him on the back and said, "It's over. You can calm down now."

"Sir, I've never shot at anyone before."

"Then you know what it'll be like if you have to do it again," said Slocum.

"Heaven forbid, sir."

"I hope you're right."

Slocum carried the carbine down to the passenger walkway, where he met O'Malley.

"You surely do use that well, son," said O'Malley. "Thank you."

"We have a problem," said Slocum. "I seem to have killed the two men who knew what this was all about."

"Once we get the bales aboard again, we can search through them. I don't figure duPont and Martin would go to all that effort unless they knew which bales they wanted."

"I don't think so. They might know the general section

of cargo," said Slocum, "but I think Sam Jackson was the only one who knew precisely where the contraband was hidden."

"So we find it," said O'Malley, shrugging. The old man grimaced with pain as he moved.

"I want to learn everything. Who is involved, how Sam Jackson got into this, all the details. And I want to know who killed him. He was my friend."

O'Malley looked skeptical about Slocum ferreting out anything more than what the illicit cargo was, but he said nothing.

"There's one other person who knows," said Slocum.

This pulled O'Malley around, eyes narrowed. "Who?"

Slocum said nothing. Rather than tending to his wound, Captain O'Malley trailed along behind Slocum as he made his way to the stateroom on the far side of the ballroom, next to the captain's cabin.

"Mr. Slocum," said O'Malley, "you had better know what you're doing."

"I think I do," said Slocum.

He knocked on the cabin door. Eleanore answered.

"John, is it over?" The brunette looked him over for more wounds. When she saw none, her attention turned to Captain O'Malley. "You're hurt. Let me..." Eleanore was pushed aside by Mrs. Hortense.

"Sean, you dear man. You're hurt. Let me tend your wound."

O'Malley glanced over at Slocum. The old man's shoulders slumped.

"Mrs. Hortense, we'd like to speak to you," said Slocum. Before she answered, he pushed into her stateroom.

"Young man, I did *not* invite you in."

"He's the owner of the riverboat, Mrs. Hortense," Eleanore tried to explain.

"That's no reason for him to be rude."

"For someone responsible for so many deaths, you have no claim on polite society, Mrs. Hortense."

"Sir! I protest!" The portly woman pulled herself up to her full five-foot-two height and shoved out her ample chest. None of it impressed Slocum.

"You, Martin, and duPont were in cahoots. What was it you were after? It has to be enough to kill for."

"John, Mrs. Hortense's condition! You'll excite her!"

"Excite her, hell," snapped Slocum. "She had Sam Jackson killed. Her and Martin. Who actually pulled the trigger, Mrs. Hortense?"

"Two men Berton hired," she said sullenly.

"Berton? Berton Fellows?" Eleanore Dahlquist put one slender hand to her mouth. "You and the lawyer?"

"Her and the lawyer," said Slocum. "And Martin and duPont. There was an army of them, each guiltier than the other. Fellows had Sam Jackson gunned down, and I almost died with him. The rest of it—all that's happened aboard the *Excalibur*—is Mrs. Hortense's doing. Isn't it?" he said to the woman.

She nodded, her mouth set in a thin line.

"But why?" asked O'Malley. "I thought we, you . . . hell!"

"You're a nice man, Sean, but not too bright. You have no ambition," Mrs. Hortense said. "He gave you command of a riverboat again, and you'd found your heaven on earth. I want more. I could never be happy sailing this miserable mud ribbon up and down."

"But, Mrs. Hortense, you?" Eleanore Dahlquist gasped.

"Oh, shut up, Eleanore. You're as stupid as Sean. All you could do was take up with the likes of *him*." She sniffed as she looked condescendingly at Slocum.

"Mrs. Hortense has been a busy lady," said Slocum. "But I want the details."

"I've admitted Berton had your friend murdered. What more do you want?" the portly woman demanded.

"You can start with what it is that's got men killing one another."

Mrs. Hortense said nothing.

"Why, Mrs. Hortense?" asked Eleanore, still stunned that

her employer was responsible for all the carnage.

"My dear, the War wiped out my daddy's plantation. I only sought to get back what was rightfully mine."

"You're not from a Northern manufacturing family?" Eleanore shook her head as if something had come loose inside.

"Hardly. Damn Yankees!"

"We agree on that, at least," said Slocum. "Let me guess. You lost your family estate. You weren't going to St. Louis for any sick husband. You were going there to arrange for the sale of whatever it was that Sam Jackson smuggled North." The expression on her piglike face told Slocum he was right.

"Mrs. Hortense, you'd better not say anything more. You can get a lawyer—Mr. Fellows—and—"

"Shut up, Eleanore," said Mrs. Hortense, without a hint of rancor.

Eleanore clung to Slocum.

"She's not going to say any more," said Captain O'Malley. "I'll put a steward outside her door and keep him on guard. She won't escape."

"There's no need for that, Captain," said Slocum. "Mrs. Hortense has nowhere to go." He silently added, *Neither do any of the rest of us. The War made certain of that.* Even as he despised her for what she had done to his friend, he understood the hopelessness driving her.

"Very well. Mr. Slocum, a word with you?" O'Malley indicated he wanted to go outside into the ballroom.

Slocum pulled Eleanore along with him. O'Malley frowned when he saw the brunette, then ignored her totally. "I want to find this contraband immediately. I am tired of being shot at, kidnapped, and having my crew mutiny."

"What will you do with it when you find it?" asked Slocum.

"That depends on what it is. I am interested only in the welfare of the *Excalibur* and its crew and passengers. This contraband is jeopardizing my sacred trust."

Slocum might have laughed at this earlier. Not now. He knew Sean O'Malley well enough to know the captain meant it. He had been given a new lease on life when he had been offered command of the *Excalibur*. Nothing else mattered to him.

"Let's cut open some cotton bales," said Slocum. Eleanore stayed at his elbow all the way forward to where Erasmus Washington and the others had finished the chore of re-loading the bales.

"That will be all, Mr. Washington," said the captain. "If there is anything else, we'll call you."

Washington nodded, reluctant to leave. But Slocum wasn't going to counter the captain's orders. The fewer who knew what was hidden inside the bales, the better.

He, O'Malley, and Eleanore began cutting and digging, starting with the bales Martin had ordered put dockside first. Slocum ripped into the interior of four bales before he found the small chest.

He cut away more of the fibrous long-staple cotton and pulled out the chest, dropping it to the deck. Inside lay the reason for Sam Jackson's death, the government agent's murder, and all the rest.

"Well, open it, man," said O'Malley.

"John?" asked Eleanore. "Should you? Maybe you'd best find the authorities and..."

Slocum found a prybar and jerked off the lock. The flimsy lid snapped back to reveal neat stacks of greenbacks.

"There must be ten thousand dollars there," whispered O'Malley.

Slocum frowned. This wasn't the answer. It couldn't be. Berton Fellows had offered almost twice this for the *Excalibur*'s cargo. There was more. There had to be.

13

"Here's another one," said Eleanore Dahlquist, her voice quaking with emotion. She clutched the box as if it would explode. "How much do you suppose this makes?"

Slocum had no idea. After they had found the chest laden with the Yankee greenbacks, he had insisted on searching further. The next cotton bale had contained a parcel of scrip wrapped in oilskin. And the next and the next and the one following that. Out of ten bales checked, Slocum had retrieved six parcels of money.

"This is more money'n I've seen in my whole damn life," said Sean O'Malley. He ran his fingers over the tightly wrapped packages of money.

"More than we've all seen in this lifetime," said Slocum. He perched on the edge of a crate, thinking hard. Sam Jackson had no reason to smuggle the money like this unless there was something illegal about it. Stolen? Slocum would have heard of a train or bank robbery this large. Even a government payroll wouldn't amount to this huge mound of greenbacks, either. Most army posts paid in gold.

There had to be more than a hundred thousand dollars in the stash, all twenties.

Slocum couldn't think of any way this money might have come into his friend's hands legally, but any illegal act would have caused ripples everyone would be talking about.

"All so crisp and new," said Eleanore, running her finger over a bundle. The longing in her voice caught Slocum's attention as much as her words. She had been down on her luck since the War—who hadn't?—and she saw this as a way out.

"Read me a serial number," Slocum said.

"The little number down in the corner?" Eleanore slowly recited it. Slocum and O'Malley nodded when she did so. "What's wrong?" Eleanore asked. "You two look as if everything were crystal clear."

"It is," said Slocum.

"Well, it isn't to me. Please explain." The way she spoke told Slocum she wasn't going to like the explanation for all this money, either.

"My dear," spoke up Captain O'Malley, "I fear this is not money."

"Of course it is. Look at it!" Her slender fingers stroked lovingly over the bills.

"It *looks* real," said Slocum, "but it's not. It's counterfeit. All the serial numbers are identical. It looks as if Sam Jackson got caught up in shipping counterfeit bills north to St. Louis for distribution."

"And they killed the poor lad for it," said O'Malley. He shook his head. The captain took a pipe from his jacket pocket, tapped out the bowl, and reloaded it with a fresh plug of tobacco. He struck a lucifer and started to apply it to the tobacco, then paused, smiling.

"I have always wanted to do this," O'Malley said. He pulled a twenty from the stack in Eleanore's hand. The woman emitted a tiny shriek as O'Malley lit the edge of the bill and used it to light his pipe. He inhaled deeply, thick blue clouds of smoke rising to halo his head.

Slocum stared at the money, reconstructing how it came to be here.

"There are too many people willing to kill for this," Slocum said slowly. He started to heave a wrapped bundle of it into the river, then held back. The money would float, someone would find it, and that would start a new round of searching, speculation, and murder.

"But how is Mrs. Hortense involved?" asked Eleanore. "She wouldn't know anything about counterfeiting."

"You don't know anything about her," said O'Malley, puffing furiously. "She might be the one who ran the presses."

"I don't think so," Slocum said. "She and Fellows are involved. I suspect she found out about Sam transporting the money and told the lawyer. Fellows decided to deal himself in and Sam said no, so they had him killed."

"But duPont and Martin? Where do those laddie bucks fit in?" O'Malley looked as if he were enjoying himself immensely.

"Hired by Fellows, probably. Someone aboard the *Excalibur* had to watch after the money, or find where Sam Jackson had hidden it. From the way Martin acted, they figured it was in the cotton bales, but they didn't know which ones."

"They were unloading all the cotton?"

"Why not, Eleanore? Mrs. Hortense was along to watch after her and Fellows's share. DuPont and Martin hired the roustabouts in New Orleans to help them in case of trouble, but they were only hired hands, working for a fifty-dollar bonus and nothing else."

"Clever bastards, duPont and Martin. They would pay off their flunkeys with counterfeit money."

Slocum had to agree.

"I can't believe Mrs. Hortense is involved, yet she is. I heard it with my own ears." Eleanore looked grief-stricken. Slocum knew the only thing that would console the woman was scattered in piles around their feet.

And that would cause nothing but trouble. Fellows still expected his money. Worst of all, James Poindexter had been murdered. Slocum had no idea which man was responsible. Probably duPont, since Martin and Mrs. Hortense had been together at the time, but it didn't matter. A government Treasury agent had been brutally killed. Slocum reckoned the Yankee law wouldn't take kindly to having one of its own slaughtered in such a fashion.

It might be possible to alibi and say the agent had got drunk and fallen overboard, but Slocum doubted this would satisfy anyone. His superiors had to know Poindexter was on the trail of counterfeiters and would suspect foul play. When they discovered Sam Jackson had been murdered, that duPont and Martin and half a dozen others of the *Excalibur* crew were also dead, that would be the final straw.

Slocum wanted to avoid such scrutiny at all costs. It wouldn't take more than a few days for them to find out about the carpetbagger judge decaying in a lonely grave back in Georgia.

"There's been nothing but trouble over this money," said Slocum, "but I don't know what we can do with it."

"How many more bales do we have to go through?" asked O'Malley. "I feel in my bones that there must be more."

Slocum thought of Berton Fellows' offer. If the lawyer and Mrs. Hortense intended to sell this worthless paper for a few cents on the dollar to get a wider distribution, that meant even as much as a hundred dollars might not be all. Two hundred thousand? More? Sold for as little as ten cents on the dollar, that would be close to Fellows's break-even offer.

"Captain, we'll keep looking. You go tend to getting the boiler fixed."

O'Malley eyed Slocum. "You're not thinking of jumping ship with all this, are you, son?"

"No. I don't know what I'm going to do with it. Not only is it counterfeit, it's got more blood on it than I care to think about."

O'Malley silently turned and vanished in the maze of crates and cotton bales on the deck. Slocum and Eleanore went back to work slashing open the canvas-packed cotton and rooting about like hungry sows looking for kernels of corn in slop. By the time they'd finished more than an hour later, over four hundred thousand in the bogus scrip had been stacked knee-high on the forward deck.

"So much money," sighed Eleanore, "and none of it is real."

"Don't sound so wistful. It's got to be destroyed in such a way that the Treasury agents are satisfied."

"But there's so much. It . . . it *feels* nice, John." Eleanore ran her fingers over the intricate engraving. Ink smudged off as she stroked. She wiped the green and black ink off onto a wad of cotton.

"Help me put it into this tarp." Slocum and Eleanore piled all the counterfeit scrip in the center of a large tarpaulin. Slocum pulled the edges in and secured them with a length of wire from a cotton bale. It made a hefty bundle. He swung it up and onto his shoulder, then lugged it back to the edge of the cargo deck. Below stood the boilers where Macallum and his engineers toiled to get the blown plate riveted back into place.

From above came Erasmus Washington's booming bass:

"Oh, I wouldn't be a fireman,
  He works amid the coal,
  I'd rather be a gamblin' man,
  That wears a ring of gold."

"He does sing beautifully," Eleanore said, looking up at the roustabout lounging on the stairs leading up to the passengers' walkway. "I heard tell of a captain on another boat. Captain Cushing, I think his name was."

"What about him?"

"He was an opera singer in New York City. He'd serenade his passengers as he piloted up the river. Must have been interesting."

"Never cared much for opera," Slocum said. "I'll take Ras' singing any day."

"Mr. Slocum! That you?" came Sean O'Malley's cry from below. "I'd have a word with you."

"Be right back, Eleanore," he told the woman. He didn't have to add that he wanted her to watch the sack of scrip.

Slocum dropped the bundle of money and went to the boiler deck, avoiding the cordwood the engineers had scattered to get to the damaged boiler.

"How are the repairs progressing, Captain?" he asked.

"Well, son, very well. Mr. Macallum is a fine engineer." O'Malley pointed. Macallum swarmed over the boiler, hammering and putting the finishing touches on the ruptured plate. "We can be up to steam within an hour. I'll be more than happy to once more see nothing but water around the *Excalibur*. I do not enjoy being tied down to a dock."

"We'll all be a sight happier when we arrive in St. Louis," Slocum said.

Slocum had just started up from the boiler deck when the pilot, Smithson, shouted down from the texas deck, "Captain! In the river! To our stern!"

O'Malley hurried to look; so did Slocum.

"Can we never be free of those bastards?" cried O'Malley. "I'm beginning to believe the stories that the *Excalibur* is cursed."

"Get the other boilers up to steam," ordered Slocum. "The *Excalibur* can outrun a keelboat."

"It takes us a powerful long time to get this bulk moving, and against the current..." O'Malley shrugged and held his hands out to indicate the futility.

"Do it. I will not sit and do nothing while they board us. We fought them off once. We can do it again. But I'd as soon outrun them."

"Mr. Macallum can do wonders," allowed O'Malley, "but miracles might be beyond his range."

Slocum let the captain tend to getting the engines running again. He grabbed Eleanore by the arm and pushed her up the stairs toward the passenger deck.

"Get up there and stay out of the way if shooting starts," he told her.

"No, John. I want to be with you."

"You want to make sure I don't make off with the money," Slocum accused. The expression on Eleanore's face told him this was part of it, too. In a way he didn't blame her. She had been treated poorly by fate until now. Eleanore saw the future in terms of having enough money. With damn near five hundred thousand in fake twenties tempting her, even a saint might get a mite suspicious of him.

"There's going to be trouble. The river pirates," he said, pointing. "They're not giving up as easy as I'd hoped."

"But if Mrs. Hortense hired them, why can't she tell them to quit?"

"Come on." Slocum pulled the brunette behind him like a fish on a line. He nodded to the steward standing guard outside the matron's stateroom. Inside, Mrs. Hortense sat in a large chair, hunched over and looking very, very small. She didn't even glance up as Slocum and Eleanore came in.

"Mrs. Hortense, are they treating you all right?" Eleanore thought the woman might have been physically tortured into such despair.

"You little fool! You've ruined everything!" Mrs. Hortense accused. "You couldn't be content with working for me. You had to take up with *him.*"

"The river pirates are going to be trying to board the *Excalibur* in a few minutes," Slocum said. "You can wave them off."

"Pirates?" The woman snorted derisively. "Those were duPont's doing. Leander and I argued over it. He thought it was a fine idea. I disputed that. No, Mr. Slocum, those cutthroats do not work for me."

"Just the ones who murdered Sam Jackson," he muttered.

Even as he spoke, Slocum knew he was getting nowhere.

"Mrs. Hortense, how could you do these awful things?" Eleanore dropped to her knees in front of the woman and clutched at a flabby arm. Mrs. Hortense pulled away.

"What do you know? We were rich. Before the War, we were rich. My daddy had the largest plantation in all of eastern Louisiana. Mr. Hortense, damn his eyes, always had the wild schemes. He cost me the plantation. Even with the War, we could have held onto it."

Slocum stared at the woman. Finally, he said, "Your husband was responsible for the counterfeiting?"

"During the War, he convinced that ass Trenholm that printing the counterfeit money would undermine the Yankees' efforts."

Slocum nodded. George Trenholm hadn't been the wisest man in Jeff Davis's cabinet. The position of Secretary of the Treasury had been beyond him in many ways. Not content with managing the considerable finances, he had dabbled in the war effort in many other ways. This struck Slocum as being something that would have been attempted by the man.

"The money was hidden away," said Slocum, "on your plantation, where you could get at it."

"We were driven off the plantation," Mrs. Hortense said bitterly. "Somehow, Sam Jackson got wind of the money and removed it. Berton and I wanted it back, but Sam Jackson wouldn't have any of it. He said it was all his, fair and square."

Slocum saw how intricate the dealings had become. The money had been printed and lost at the end of the War, then recovered by Sam Jackson. Mrs. Hortense and Fellows had done all in their power to steal it back and had failed. That duPont and Martin lay dead gave mute testimony to that.

"Go to your room, Eleanore, and keep the door closed. Don't let anyone in."

"But, John!"

He escorted her from Mrs. Hortense's room. "Do it.

We're going to have to try to repel the pirates again. They want the money and they will kill us to get it."

Even as he spoke, a window in the ballroom shattered, the bullet whistling up to bury itself in the ornate ceiling. Slocum rushed to his room, grabbed his spare Colt, and returned to the walkway, not even looking to see if Eleanore obeyed. Once again, they were in a fight for their lives.

A few river pirates from the lead keelboat tried to board the *Excalibur* and found Erasmus Washington and his baling hook too formidable to oppose. Slocum fired four times, quick, and dropped one pirate who managed to get aboard and who crept up on the tall black roustabout.

"Thank you, Mistuh Slocum," Washington called, never breaking his motion as he swung the deadly baling hook back and forth in front of him. He caught one pirate under the chin and lifted him bodily into the air. But it cost Ras the hook as the man twisted, his weight jerking the hook from Washington's hand.

"You need this, Mr. Slocum?" came a steady voice. Slocum turned to see Smithson beside him, the heavy Spencer carbine in his hand. The young pilot passed it across. "I took the liberty of loading it for you, sir."

Slocum curtly nodded, flipped up the hind sights, and went to work. Four careful shots found four pirates.

As he fired, he gave orders. "Smithson, get up to the pilot house. Get us out into the river. It's our only chance." Coming around the bend in the river were three more keelboats crammed to the gunwales with men shouting obscenities and waving knives and pistols. If even one of those boats joined the one already grappled to the *Excalibur,* all was lost.

They had to outrun the pirates. Nothing else would save them.

Slocum heard the pilot's boots on the stairs leading up. He fired again, the heavy carbine smashing into his shoulder. While he missed, the nearness of the bullet passing over one man's head sent him crashing to the deck, dazed.

Ras Washington kicked the man in the side and shoved him into the water. By this time others had joined Washington, but the battle slowly went against them. Tired and dispirited from duPont's abortive takeover of the *Excalibur*, the roustabouts hardly fought the pirates now.

Captain O'Malley shouted orders, but most were directed at Macallum and his engineers. Slocum heard steam hissing through pipes and felt the deep shudders as the *Excalibur* built up a head to once more become the floating city it was. But the keelboats pushed closer and closer, the pirates jeering and beginning to shoot, even though the distance was still too great for a handgun.

Slocum glanced over the edge of the deck and saw the firemen sweating to get enough wood into the boilers. The huge lengths of wood did not catch fire quickly enough; something more volatile was required to get the temperatures high enough to ignite the four-foot lengths of wood.

"Captain!" he shouted. "Use the cotton. There!"

O'Malley instantly saw what Slocum meant. The man nodded and started lugging some of the ripped-open bales toward the edge of the deck. He shoved it over onto the boiler deck for the firemen and went to get another.

Slocum fired his carbine, knocked the pirate back into the keelboat, then just stood, eyes fixed on the tarp laden with the counterfeit money.

"John, no, please don't!" came Eleanore's impassioned cry from the passenger deck. Slocum rested his rifle against a railing and went to the tarp. Straining, he dragged it to the edge. O'Malley came up beside him with another armful of cotton.

"Is this what you want to do, son?" the old man asked.

"We need steam in a hurry. The cotton's not getting it for us."

"It does solve some of our problems," O'Malley admitted. The captain helped him lift the makeshift bag up and drop it over to the firemen. Macallum ducked out of the way as it smashed down, then moved it to the gaping mouth of the furnace. He and a fireman tossed the tarp into the blazing fire.

One of the firemen stopped and pointed when a handful of the twenties spilled out. As the man bent to pick up the counterfeit bills, Macallum kicked him in the butt and yelled at him to get to work.

After that, no one stopped to gawk. They worked with a vengeance to build the temperature. Slocum ran to the aft of the boat when he saw the long lengths of cordwood going into the furnace and starting to burn almost instantly. The boilers were generating their share of steam now. The huge paddlewheels churned sluggishly.

Washington and the few crewmen still fighting had their hands full. The pirates swarmed like bees from a kicked hive now. Slocum showed no mercy. At point-blank range, he fired the .55 caliber carbine with an accuracy that disheartened the pirates. But they showed no indication of retreating; reinforcements were only a few hundred yards distant, and closing the gap faster and faster.

If any of those three additional boatloads grappled onto the *Excalibur,* all was lost.

"Ras, get that bale of cotton over to the edge. There." Slocum saw Washington's muscles strain as the man singlehandedly moved the huge bale. Slocum vaulted to the cargo deck and ran to where Washington wrestled with another of the pirates. Slocum smashed the boarder in the back of the head with the butt of his carbine, then handed it to Washington. Slocum pulled out a lucifer and struck it. The smell of sulfur filled the air as he applied it to the side of the cotton bale.

Several of the crew gasped; nothing frightened a river man more than fire. As the flames engulfed the bale, Slocum shoved it hard with his foot. It moved a fraction of an inch.

"Heah, Mistuh Slocum. Let me do that." Washington pushed hard and the bale tumbled over the edge, falling into the keelboat. The sparks from the drifting cotton fibers spread over the pirate boat, sending the ones still aboard into the river. Their screams echoed for miles.

Slocum and Ras turned back to getting rid of the pirates still aboard. Seeing their boat fired had taken some of the determination out of them.

"One last shot," said Slocum, checking his carbine. "Got to make it count." He sighted it on the keelboat closest to the *Excalibur*. The huge gun bucked and a piece of hull the size of his fist blew out of the side. This wouldn't sink the keelboat, but it would slow it down and give the *Excalibur* desperately needed time.

"Mr. Slocum," came O'Malley's voice, "we are up to half steam. We will make it!"

The *Excalibur*'s paddles turned faster now, churning the muddy river water to white froth. The keelboat no longer overtook the riverboat. The pirates shot at the *Excalibur* and cursed. Someone got careless and ran their boat into the keelboat blazing all the way down to the waterline. This cost them precious minutes. By the time they had avoided the other sinking pirate boat, the hole Slocum had put in their hull had allowed in enough water to cause the boat to list heavily. The other two boats fell farther and farther back.

Slocum heaved a sigh and sat down, staring at the pirates. Within ten minutes O'Malley had the *Excalibur* up to full speed. At a steady thirteen miles an hour, no pirates' keelboat could keep up.

"We escaped, John," said Eleanore, standing behind him, her hand resting on his shoulder. "And the money is all gone."

Slocum looked at the coroneted escape pipes spewing forth their black smoke. "It was money well spent," he said. "It bought us our lives."

Slocum had to laugh at Eleanore's expression, but he shared some of her sadness, too. That was a powerful lot of money to shovel into a furnace, even if it had been counterfeit.

14

Slocum and Eleanore Dahlquist stood on the texas deck looking upriver. The Lombardy poplars gave the pilot Smithson guideposts for navigating the treacherous Mississippi, and the trip had progressed smoothly after evading the pirates and fixing the boiler.

"It's a pity," said Eleanore.

"About the counterfeit money?" Slocum puffed the last of his havana and flicked the butt far over the side. The faint ember left an orange trail in the gathering dusk. He imagined he heard the hiss as the coal hit the water. That wasn't possible over the heavy churning of the paddle-wheels.

"What else?" The brunette sounded bitter.

Crewmen came to drop curtains over the skylights opening onto the ballroom and canvas already covered the forward ports on the boiler deck. Absolute dark was required for the pilot to be able to see in the darkness. Slocum wanted another havana but this, too, was forbidden. Some things even the *Excalibur*'s owner didn't argue over. The idea of running aground when they'd been through so much didn't set well with him. If he wanted to smoke, he could go below. For the moment, however, he was content to stand, arm circling Eleanore's waist, and simply look at the rays of the setting sun reflecting redly off the rippling waters and then dying to inky blackness. Bats fluttered out to scoop from the humid air their fill of buzzing, humming insects. Lightning bugs flashed on and off, then vanished, prey to the erratically flying bats.

"It's lovely, John," the woman said. "I wish this could go on forever."

"It can't. St. Louis isn't that far-away. By midday tomorrow, Captain O'Malley says."

"He's such a dear," said Eleanore. "The way he's treating Mrs. Hortense shows that."

Slocum said nothing. He figured that O'Malley loved the conniving woman, and it had cut deeply when she had turned out to be involved in so many murders. Not that she'd pulled the trigger herself, but she had used the old man, and that hurt his pride. Slocum knew O'Malley might have been able to forgive Mrs. Hortense, even if she had killed Jackson and the others, but that was impossible now that she had used him. Dignity and honor were all O'Malley had when he came aboard the *Excalibur*. He had regained a measure of respect by his hard-nosed, fair captaincy, but the woman had cut to the heart of all he held precious.

Slocum understood that. He had damn little but his own sense of honor left.

"You still going to sign over the *Excalibur* to Marie Jackson?" Eleanore snuggled closer, her hip rubbing suggestively against his.

"Yes. By all rights, it's hers. She might not have liked the way Jackson lived or the river or anything about the *Excalibur*, but it's hers."

"You could be rich if you kept it."

"Wouldn't feel right keeping Sam's legacy. This belongs to his widow. I wasn't much more'n a caretaker for it."

"You did a good job. You could have accepted Berton Fellows's offer to agent the boat. That was almost two thousand dollars."

Slocum didn't mind having money. The fancy clothes he had bought out of the *Excalibur*'s operating funds hung on his back. The food had been good. Being with Eleanore had been damn good, too. But there wasn't the sense of freedom he needed. Playing at being the owner of the *Excalibur* tied him down in ways that tore at him. He had to make decisions on the day-to-day operation of the riverboat that were beyond the captain or the pilot. Even though he was going to turn the boat over to Sam's widow when they docked, Slocum took the job seriously.

"I got all I need," he said. He kissed Eleanore. The woman returned the kiss fervently, then pushed away from him.

"Let me go below. Give me...oh, give me an hour. Then join me. Will you, John?"

"Why wait so long? An hour can be longer'n eternity waiting for a woman like you."

"Then you'll just have to endure it," she said, smiling. "It'll be special, John. I promise."

"With you, it's always special." Eleanore brushed her lips against his cheek, then turned and left the texas deck with a rustle of her dress. Slocum leaned over the railing and peered into the night-cloaked distance. How Smithson saw a damn thing was beyond him. Tiny ripples showed here and there on the river surface, but they weren't sandbars. Or were they? Slocum didn't know, but the young pilot did. He earned the five hundred a month he was paid for this demanding chore.

Slocum gripped the railing harder as the rudders turned and sent the *Excalibur* farther toward the middle of the river, avoiding the ripples he had spotted. Only when the boat was abreast of the offending spot did Slocum see the submerged sandbar that would have delayed them long hours if they'd run aground.

The trip had been anything but dull, but landing at the docks in St. Louis would provide even more excitement. Slocum believed that James Poindexter had been required to send cables at certain stops along the river. When those cables never arrived at the other end of the *Excalibur's* route, it had to have alerted Treasury agents. Slocum envisioned a dock lined with the men dressed in their coats, bowler hats, and sawed-off shotguns.

The chance existed that Poindexter had even recognized Slocum as a judge killer, but had refrained from doing anything until he found the counterfeit Yankee scrip. With the bogus money turned to cinder and ash in the *Excalibur's* furnaces—the best use for it Slocum could find, since it got the two massive engines up to full power and pulled them away from the pirates—the Treasury agents might be even more skeptical about letting him walk away.

After all, he was still owner of the *Excalibur* and responsible for much that had happened.

"Mr. Slocum," the pilot called out, "could I trouble you to find Captain O'Malley? I need some assistance."

Slocum nodded and left the deck. He still had more than half an hour till he found the paradise Eleanore had promised him. He walked slowly to the passenger deck and along the walkway. Erasmus Washington sang a baleful tune from the stern, with other deckhands joining in. Slocum felt a twinge at knowing how he'd miss this. No matter what happened in St. Louis, he wouldn't be making the return trip down the Mississippi on the *Excalibur*.

He ducked into the ballroom and went to the bar. The bartender had done well this trip, being an independent businessman.

"What'll it be, Mr. Slocum?" the barkeep asked. "A French brandy?"

Slocum shook his head. The vile concoction would rot his innards faster than anything he'd ever downed. The barkeep had just burned another peach stone for it. The rest of the ingredients were spread out along the bar: cod liver oil, nitric acid, and cheap Kentucky whiskey.

"Make it rye." A gleaming shotglass appeared magically in front of him and the barkeep deftly filled it. Slocum took a sip, decided he had got the good bottle, then knocked it back in a single quick gulp. The whiskey burned all the way to his belly, where it formed a pool and settled in for a long stay. It made Slocum feel easier.

Leaving all this splendor wasn't going to be simple for him.

Slocum glanced around the large ballroom, then smiled slightly. He had time. He dropped the empty glass onto the bar and left quickly. No one saw him as he quietly slipped down to the cargo deck. He went forward to where the steam crane had been set up once more in preparation for the unloading tomorrow afternoon.

His long, slender-bladed knife gleamed briefly in the light of the quarter-moon. There were dozens of cotton bales that they hadn't searched.

Slocum returned to his stateroom, cleaned up a mite, then went to Eleanore's cabin. He didn't bother knocking. He went in to find the woman already in bed wearing nothing more than a smile.

"Are you sure you want to do this, son?" asked O'Malley. The old man scratched his head. "She's guilty as sin, her and this lawyer. They can be tried for murder."

"I'll take care of Fellows myself," said Slocum. "Maybe no time soon, but I know who was responsible for killing Jackson. He won't get away with it."

"Might be easier, at that," admitted Sean O'Malley. "The authorities ask so many damn fool questions—and you're not wanting that, are you?"

Slocum didn't answer.

"Very well. We'll put into St. Louis about noontime, but you'll be put off the *Excalibur* a few hours earlier. Will I see you again?"

"I don't know, Captain. Where I'm going is wide open

spaces. The river's nice enough for travelling, but it's not home for me like it is for you."

O'Malley stared at Slocum without speaking. He held out his hand and shook it. Slocum knew all the things O'Malley wanted to say but couldn't, and that suited him fine. He didn't need the old man's thanks for giving him another chance to prove he was a good river man.

Slocum picked up his single heavy bag and went to the stern where a small boat bobbed and bounced in the *Excalibur*'s wake. Erasmus Washington waited there for him.

"Is this just coincidence, Mr. Washington?"

"No, suh, can't say that it is. Figured you'd be leavin' us 'fore we docked and that it'd be in this heah boat. You want me to row you ashore?"

"Thanks, Ras, but that won't be necessary. I may be the owner, but I can still do my own rowing."

"Not owner for long." Washington obviously didn't cotton to the idea of still another owner. And rumors had already travelled the length and breadth of the *Excalibur* that Slocum was turning over the title of ownership to Jackson's widow.

"She'll keep Captain O'Malley on," said Slocum. "She won't want to do anything but spend the cash the *Excalibur* makes for her." Sean O'Malley had told Slocum that, in spite of all the delays and problems, the *Excalibur* had made almost five thousand dollars' profit for the trip from New Orleans. The captain had chuckled saying that they'd saved on the twelve thousand in salaries by not paying the five hundred a month coming to Alexander duPont or the two hundred a month owed Leander Martin.

"The others might be right about this being a jinxed boat and you being a jinxed owner," said Washington, "but it ain't been dull, I'll give it that." The man pointed to the tiny rowboat.

Slocum slapped Ras on the shoulder, dropped his heavy bag into the boat, and followed it. Washington cast off for him and Slocum found himself fighting to stay upright in the tiny boat as the wash from the *Excalibur*'s paddles hit. He rowed for all he was worth and got free of the turbulence. Slocum didn't care to row against the current so he angled back toward the shore, letting the sluggishly flowing river help him along.

For an instant Slocum thought he spotted Eleanore Dahlquist at the stern with Erasmus Washington, but he knew he had to be mistaken. The night with the lovely brunette had been delightful, but he had not told her he was leaving in this fashion. It would have upset her too much and caused complications.

When the Treasury men questioned her, Eleanore could truthfully tell them she had no idea where he'd gone.

It was better this way.

Slocum put his back into the rowing and reached the muddy west bank in less than thirty minutes. It took another thirty for him to work out the kinks in his back from the effort and another hour to find a farmer willing to sell him a swaybacked plug horse that had seen better days before the War. As sorry as the animal was, it felt good to be back astride a horse; it was where he belonged. He kicked at the animal's flanks and headed for St. Louis.

Slocum spent the afternoon asking around to find someone who knew where Marie Jackson lived. He hadn't wanted to go down dockside when the *Excalibur* had put in because of the rumors circulating about U. S. Government men swarming over the riverboat. It had been just as Slocum had foreseen. If he had stayed with the *Excalibur* there wouldn't have been any way off without being questioned. And they had to be mighty pissed off about losing one of their own.

Slocum didn't doubt that Mrs. Hortense would play along and keep her mouth shut. Martin and duPont would be blamed for everything, no one would know a thing about the counterfeit money, and, if asked, the chief engineer could tell about the bales of cotton shoved into the furnaces to give them added steam power to get away from the river pirates.

The Treasury agents would not believe that, but there'd be little else they could do except watch the *Excalibur* and its crew for any sign of the bogus greenbacks.

Slocum smiled. It would be wasted effort on their part, and on Berton Fellows's part, too. The money was gone up in smoke, through the furnace and up the coroneted chimney pipes standing above the majestic *Excalibur*.

"Heard about Jackson," one river man told him in a dockside saloon. Slocum wondered how the news had travelled upriver this fast, but said nothing. "Pity. Sam was a good man. Fine captain, but a little lenient with his crew. Let the bastards get by with murder. Even fed the roustabouts from other'n the 'grub pile,' I heard tell once." The man shook his head vigorously. "No way to run a boat."

Slocum bought the man another drink. "Heard tell Sam's widow is a right pretty woman. Where might I go to pay my condolences?" The river man misunderstood, as Slocum had figured he would. That didn't matter. Slocum got the information he needed without attracting too much unwanted attention. He paid, sliding a greenback across the bar, and left, the change jingling in his pocket.

Marie Jackson lived in a modest frame house a dozen miles from the dock area. Slocum tethered his plow horse to the whitewashed picket fence and went up the neatly tended path. Flowers bloomed sporadically and the constant hum of bees filled the air. He knocked on the door and waited until the smallish, tired-looking woman answered.

"Mrs. Jackson?" he asked.

She bobbed her head up and down, not speaking. Slocum told her his story.

She seemed reluctant to allow him into her tidy, quiet home, but she finally relented. Slocum felt uncomfortable perched on the edge of a chair, sipping at the coffee she had fixed for him.

"So you're just giving me the *Excalibur?* I find this hard to believe, Mr. Slocum."

"Sam was a friend of mine back in Georgia. The boat's not rightly mine."

"You don't have to do this."

"It's right. It's what Sam would have wanted, if he'd had the time to do it. Here." Slocum pulled out the title to the boat and hastily filled in the spaces transferring ownership to the woman. She barely glanced at it.

"Sam's gone. I'd trade a hundred riverboats to get him back."

"You haven't asked how he died. Did you hear already? The dockside rumors?"

"There have been many men here. One of them told me."

Slocum went cold inside when he heard that. The only ones who might have come by like this worked either for Berton Fellows or the Treasury Department. One was as bad as the other in his eyes.

"The *Excalibur* is legally yours. I'd say that Captain O'Malley is a fine choice to run it. He's a good captain and an honest man."

The woman shook her head at this.

"I'm sure you could find someone willing to buy it, also," Slocum went on, "if that's your wish, but O'Malley will provide you with a good income."

"Thank you for your advice, Mr. Slocum."

Slocum allowed the woman to escort him to the door. Her coldness and unconcern affected him. Marie Jackson seemed truly to miss her husband, but nothing else touched her emotionally. Slocum had seen women like this during the War. Their capacity for caring had been overloaded and they went through life, half a woman, numbed to everything but the primary loss. He hoped this woman would grow out of it, but he had seen many others who hadn't. That was one cost of dying he had no way of paying for anyone else. He wasn't even sure he'd paid it for himself yet. The loss of his brother and his parents still weighed heavy, even after four years of grieving.

The dusk had settled, but Slocum's sharp eyes and suspicions alerted him to the moving gray shadows. From behind three elm trees came men carrying shotguns.

"John Slocum, we have a warrant for your arrest. Don't try to escape."

They might have been government agents or bounty hunters. It made no difference. Somewhere Slocum had been careless and they had followed him. Or, more likely, they had been waiting for him to speak with Marie Jackson. He had tried to evade them at the docks by leaving the *Excalibur* downriver, and the trick had failed.

Slocum's hand flew to his Colt Navy. One smooth motion pulled it from his cross-draw holster and a bullet winged into the dark shadow, in the general direction of the man on his right. Slocum missed, but the bullet came close enough to bring out a string of corrosive cursing.

Bright tongues from the shotguns blindingly filled the night, but Slocum had already shifted location, diving to his right. One post on the porch erupted into splinters. The porch roof sagged down and a window shattered as buckshot pellets went in all directions.

Slocum fired again. This time he found a human target. The Treasury agent—that was who he figured these to be— limped away, cursing even louder than before. Slocum tried to lure them around to the side of the house so he could make a dash for his horse, but they wouldn't have any of it.

Their shotgun blasts kept him moving, hiding, dodging, fearing for his hide.

When he did outmaneuver them and reach the frightened horse, Slocum knew he'd lost. One of the Treasury agents stepped out from behind a tree, leveled his shotgun, and emptied both barrels into the horse's flank. The impact lifted the old horse off its feet. It fell heavily, dead before it touched the ground. Slocum bent down, scooping up his heavy bag. Running with it weighing him down would be damn near impossible, but he was going to try it, nonetheless.

"Surrender, Slocum. You're not going to get away from us. Give up!"

Out in the open, his horse dead, shotguns covering him, bag in one hand slowing him down, Slocum knew he had only two choices: fight and die, or surrender.

His hands started up when he heard the hard pounding of hooves. He glanced to one side. The Treasury agents were distracted, too, and this allowed Slocum to vault onto the back of the horse as it raced past.

Unbalanced by his bag in one hand and the Colt in the other, Slocum almost fell off from behind the rider until a hand grabbed his shirtfront and pulled him up. Shotgun pellets rained around them, and then they galloped out of range.

"You damn near got your head blown off, John. You're going to have to be more careful."

"I'll keep that in mind, Eleanore." His arm circled the woman's trim waist.

"Not so low," she said. "You'll distract me."

"I hope so."

"Should just toss you off, leave you for those Treasury agents. You didn't even say goodbye when you left the *Excalibur*."

"Figured I'd be seeing you again, though I hadn't counted on it this soon."

"You liar. And it's good for you I had the same idea they did."

"How good a mind reader are you?" he asked. She craned her head around and peered up into his green eyes.

"That makes it twice today I've read someone's mind. And I like what I read in yours."

Slocum had to allow that she did.

15

Slocum came instantly awake, green eyes darting about. Then he settled down, remembering where he was and how he had so delightfully spent the night. Beside him Eleanore Dahlquist slept, her soft breathing so different from her passionate moans and sharp cries of pleasure when they had first gone to bed. Slocum lay flat on his back, fingers laced and behind his head. He stared at the plastered hotel ceiling, thinking back over the past week.

It had been a combination of rare danger and all the erotic skills Eleanore could offer.

They had ridden from Marie Jackson's house until Eleanore's horse stumbled, fell, and broke its leg. Slocum had taken care of it with a single bullet between the eyes, but that left them afoot with the government men in hot pursuit. The feel of buckshot piercing his skin wasn't much to Slocum's liking. Neither was the idea of spending most of his life behind bars—the part of his life left before they dropped him through the trap on a gallows, a stout hemp rope around his neck.

He and Eleanore had been lucky to find the man with the wagon and team of strong horses. When they left, the man was sitting in a wagon without any animals hitched to it—and sixty dollars richer, the three twenty-dollar greenbacks clutched in his hand.

Slocum sighed. The ride had been almost as bad as the headlong flight away from Marie Jackson's house. The animals were not used to being ridden and he and Eleanore had to stay on them bareback, but they had managed.

Slocum now knew how a mouse felt when a tomcat decided on dinner. The lawmen had been merciless tracking him down, but Slocum had been just a little cagier and had kept far enough ahead to elude them. Now that a full week had passed, he figured they were looking in other directions. He and Eleanore had gone to earth and stayed, moving about on the St. Louis streets only as much as they had to.

"Ummm, John?" came the sleepy voice. Eleanore rolled over, a bare shoulder nudging against his chest. Then a naked breast rubbed against him as the woman snuggled closer.

"Time to move again," he told her. They hadn't stayed longer than two or three days at any hotel. They had been lucky, arriving at two of the hostelries after the federals had already checked out the premises. St. Louis was a big enough city that they couldn't continually check—and Slocum didn't kid himself. They wanted him for killing the carpetbagger judge and probably for counterfeiting, too, but they weren't going to make him a career. Other, easier-to-find prey existed that would make the time spent more productive.

"Now?" Eleanore wrapped both legs around Slocum's thigh and began rocking to and fro. He felt her excitement awakening. And the way she ran her fingers across his belly—and lower—brought him fully erect.

"Soon," he amended. "There's no need for us to stay in St. Louis any longer."

Eleanore caught his tone and stopped her movement. She sat up in bed, the sheet falling away to reveal her perfectly formed, snowy-white breasts. Slocum almost regretted his decision. Almost.

"We're not leaving together, are we?" she asked. "The way you said it told me that."

"I could have just left without a word. I didn't do that."

"You bastard."

"They're still after me, Eleanore. They don't even know who you are. You can lead a good life without me. With me, it'd be a constant struggle just to stay alive."

"Bullshit."

"I'm a corrupting influence. You never spoke that way before you met me."

Eleanore had to smile at that. "You're a *good* influence, John. I love you."

He'd been afraid she'd say something like that.

"It'd never work between us, Eleanore. We're two different kinds."

"I can learn. I can. Haven't we done well together this week?"

"This week. But the money's running out. I didn't win that much aboard the *Excalibur*." Slocum wondered if he kept his poker face. Not all the counterfeit money had been burned in the *Excalibur*'s furnace. He had slipped out and examined the rest of the cotton bales and found another cache of the bogus scrip. It about filled the heavy bag he carried. But Slocum knew how careful he would have to be spending the money. He'd given the wagon driver sixty dollars for the horses, and it had all been counterfeit because he hadn't the time to sort through and get legitimate bills. During the past week, also, he had learned how hard it was to pass illegal money.

He was rich, but he'd have to be wary of getting rid of it. One bill here, another there. Slowly. Carefully. Without Eleanore.

"I understand, John."

His eyes snapped around and fixed on her face. He'd never thought she would agree so quickly.

"Once more, as a parting present?" she said, lying next to him again, her body slowly moving as it had done before. He couldn't resist. Once more.

As they finished, Slocum asked, "Where will you go?"

"I was thinking of going on upriver, perhaps to Louisville. Might go north to Minneapolis for a spell. Or even east to New York."

Something in the way Eleanore spoke alerted Slocum. "How much do you have?" he asked. "I only got one other oilskin bundle."

Eleanor laughed. "I beat you to most of it, then. I found two boxes in the bales." This explained why Eleanore had wanted a full hour aboard the *Excalibur* before having Slocum join her. She hadn't been in her cabin preparing herself for him; she had been forward on the boat cutting through the tough canvas and digging inside the remaining bales for the counterfeit money they hadn't burned.

"Be careful spending it. The Treasury agents will be looking for it. And Fellows might find some way of getting more printed. That would implicate you and him."

"Don't teach your granny how to suck eggs, John Slocum. I wasn't born yesterday." Eleanore gazed into his eyes. They kissed. Reluctantly, the woman broke away. "Be careful yourself, John. Yours is the more dangerous trail."

Slocum and Eleanore found time to make love once more before they left the hotel. Slocum started to turn and look back, then stopped. He kept his back to the rising sun and walked west. By day's end he would be riding west and by week's end he would be well away from Eleanore Dahlquist, if not her pleasantly lingering memory.

But it was for the best. He had returned to the world he knew best. It suited him just fine.

GREAT WESTERN YARNS FROM ONE OF THE BEST-SELLING WRITERS IN THE FIELD TODAY

JAKE LOGAN

JAKE LOGAN

___ 0-867-21087	**SLOCUM'S REVENGE**	$1.95
___ 07296-3	**THE JACKSON HOLE TROUBLE**	$2.50
___ 07182-0	**SLOCUM AND THE CATTLE QUEEN**	$2.75
___ 06413-1	**SLOCUM GETS EVEN**	$2.50
___ 06744-0	**SLOCUM AND THE LOST DUTCHMAN MINE**	$2.50
___ 07018-2	**BANDIT GOLD**	$2.50
___ 06846-3	**GUNS OF THE SOUTH PASS**	$2.50
___ 07046-8	**SLOCUM AND THE HATCHET MEN**	$2.50
___ 07258-4	**DALLAS MADAM**	$2.50
___ 07139-1	**SOUTH OF THE BORDER**	$2.50
___ 07460-9	**SLOCUM'S CRIME**	$2.50
___ 07567-2	**SLOCUM'S PRIDE**	$2.50
___ 07382-3	**SLOCUM AND THE GUN-RUNNERS**	$2.50
___ 07494-3	**SLOCUM'S WINNING HAND**	$2.50
___ 07493-5	**SLOCUM IN DEADWOOD**	$2.50

Prices may be slightly higher in Canada.